Tangent

by
Mike Pomery

Strategic Book Publishing and Rights Co.

Strategic Book Publishing and Rights Co.
12620 FM 1960, Suite A4-507
Houston TX 77065
www.sbpra.com

ISBN: 978-1-61897-181-4

Design: Dedicated Book Services, Inc. (www.netdbs.com)

For Natasha

Hie thee hither,
That I may pour my spirits in thine ear,
And chastise with the valour of my tongue
All that impedes thee from the golden round.

—Lady Macbeth

Prologue

I suppose if I had but a modicum of intellect, I would never have agreed with his proposal.

Of all the people I've known throughout my life; I trust James the most, yet this very bias may prove to be my downfall. Never in our long friendship have I been able to discard his often fantastical musings and ideas, but this is the first time I have come rather close. I am on the cusp of throwing away immortality itself, although the final decision was always mine to make.

Such a melancholy way to start my story, I will admit to you freely. A rather dramatic introduction indeed. Allow me to apologize, dear reader, for my unintended obscurity. Let me fill in the details of this unusual moment, so as to better equip you an understanding of these sobering thoughts.

I am at present sitting in a remarkably opulent room, full of quirky antiques that crowd each corner and perch on every shelf. Heavy wooden furniture is carelessly draped with gaudy purple velvet, marring its restrained and somber beauty. The mere presence of these objects in itself is a rather quaint experience, with the flippant abandonment shown towards them only adding to the enigma. I have not seen such a collection of illegal furnishings since . . . well, since they were made illegal. That was some time ago.

Soft, flickering lamps bathe the room in a soothing amber glow. I find I cannot stop peering around me, examining the plethora of luxuriant fittings and knick knacks showing of their dusty plumage. This is despite the acute terror I am fervently attempting to ignore. My heart simply refuses to slow down to an acceptable rhythm, and no matter how many times I take a deep, steadying breath, I cannot stop the tremble of my lower lip.

Quick! Distract yourself.

Oh look; I could swear that is a genuine walnut burl humidor over there on that exquisite mahogany desk. I bet it's full of real cigars too. This genuine leather wing-back chair certainly isn't comfortable, but it sure looked regal when I was ordered to sit. Are those muskets? No, those aren't muskets.

Perhaps some quiet reflection might temporarily lift this heavy burden of dread and uncertainty? How about . . . I try and figure out why the hell I agreed to this insanity? Oh, well now we are back to the beginning of the page. Very cyclical.

I hear the soft, metallic fumble of a key scratching at a lock. Instantly, my wandering eyes snap to the heavy oak door across from me. A ponderous creak and shaft of bright light affirm an opening doorway. I shift uncomfortably in my seat and attempt to gaze nonchalantly at the silhouette standing at the threshold. I fail of course, and stare like a rabbit caught in a spotlight's beam. A soft chuckle emanates from the unmoving protagonist.

"No need to be so wary Mr. Febras," he soothes in a silky monotone. "I am sure you realize we must confine you in this room while we make preparations for your journey."

I blink stupidly in response.

He continues gently, "Please understand that we do not want you having second thoughts at such a late stage and then betraying our whereabouts to the authorities. How could we help people like you if we are locked up in prison?"

"I understand your precautions, really I do." I manage to reply somewhat placidly. "Of course you understand that it does a man no good to be alone for such a period of time, especially before such a monumental undertaking?"

"Mr. Febras . . . it has been half an hour since we last spoke." I can't see his face properly, as he is shadow-cloaked and statuesque, but I can positively hear the smile in his lips.

"Oh . . ." I retort, displaying my customary rapier wit. "It seemed much longer."

A heartier chuckle now, accompanied by a slow and studied advance from the open doorway. Took him long enough. I wager he quite enjoys putting a dramatic spin on his proceedings. He sits down on an ox-blood colored Chesterfield couch, and slowly adjusts his body until he has reached his desired level of comfort. That takes some time as well, and for a while the room is filled with sounds of squeaking leather and groaning springs. Finally, he is still. Say what you will about this man, he does things in his own time.

"Let us chat, you and I," he begins.

The bright white light flooding in from the doorway adds a sharp definition to my surrounds, and I take this moment to study his features in the now well-lit room. He is old. Impossibly old really, since you never see anyone over the age of sixty-five anymore. I consider that this may be the reason his movements have been characteristically ponderous in comparison with mine. His skin is that of an old leather jacket; wrinkled beyond decency, a map of extensive experience. He is bearded, yet well groomed, which ties in well with his immaculate three-piece brown suit. I notice that his extravagant silken-cream paisley tie in a plump Windsor knot makes his stark white hair look even paler.

I have not seen such a well dressed man in many, many years. Even his shoes are exceptionally polished and well kept. I look down at my utilitarian, composite lumps that pass as footwear these days and inwardly sigh. He regards me patiently as I awkwardly suppress a frown. As cliché as it is to state that his eyes are bright and alert, radiating intelligence and power to all that they behold, this is exactly the case.

viii   Mike Pomery

"I am Mr. Montgomery," he begins, each word clear and gentle. "You are here to take a journey with me. The purpose of this journey is to escape. You have come to the decision, one way or another, that the life offered to you at present is no longer acceptable. You may have witnessed the effects of this 'Mandatory Continuation' on those you once held dear, and have decreed that this shall not happen to you. Am I correct so far, Mr. Febras?"

"Yes," I whisper. Gone is my nervous energy, as this man's words are lancing my core with searing truths. Truths that go unuttered by any and all who surround me back home.

"Good," Mr. Montgomery acknowledges calmly. "It has long been the dream of humanity to attain immortality in some form, yet when we finally have the apparent means to do so it is at the cost of our soul. These 'Upgrades', while elevating the human body to a perfected state, destroy the very essence of life itself. You have decided that you would rather keep your soul, at the cost of denying eternal life."

He pauses to pick a ball of lint off his suit sleeve.

"This is not a light decision, Mr. Febras, but it is the right one. The unfortunate fact that it is mandatory to succumb to this abhorrent act at a specific age does little to comfort those who are not sure of the process, or the results. Such is the age we live in. Freedom, I am afraid, is a luxury only 'Criminals' like myself have."

Mr. Montgomery has an annoying habit of signaling inverted commas with his fingers, but I scarcely care at this point. I watch as he reaches over to what I had previously guessed was a humidor, and am delighted to find that I was correct. As he opens the lid, I cannot help but let out an awed gasp. It is positively crammed with cigars, almost to the point of absurdity.

He certainly is a criminal! I think to myself in derision, but admiration quickly wins out over scorn. To be caught with such taboo delights would get this eccentric old man in a lot of hot water.

He carefully selects one and picks it up gingerly, respectfully. He is actually going to *smoke* one? Ridiculous! The amount of money they would be worth is unthinkable, and it's going to go all up in smoke? I blurt this out in disbelief.

"What else am I going to do with them?" he asks in a bemused tone. "I can't stand people who collect things for the sake of owning them, and never getting around to enjoying them."

"I . . . guess so," I reply, stunned. "I used to smoke pipes before they were banned. I only had a small collection, but it was a quiet luxury that I always made time for."

Our conversation prompts me into remembering some of the simple joys that we all took for granted those many years ago, and my attitude towards Mr. Montgomery softens as I concede that maybe something other than simple eccentricity has motivated this man to acquire this forbidden, yet ultimately useless personal treasure.

"Ahh, a gentleman of refined tastes then," he says, showing signs of surprise on his weathered brow. "Would you care for one?"

"No. No thank you. I am a spot too nervous for such a thing now. I might light the head and smoke the foot in my present state of mind."

"Of course." The indulgent chuckle returns briefly. "Well, this is a 2019 Partagas Serie D Number Four. Last year of production before the famed Cuban torcedores were put out of business permanently. They are all a bit mellow now, but of course beggars can't be choosers. I used to like them within their first year. Never really got into aging them. I don't really have a choice these days though."

He has a good laugh at this, and goes about methodically cutting and lighting this rare and expensive treat. Pungent tendrils of blue smoke fill the room, and I am instantly taken back to a simpler time. Memories can be triggered by all sorts of things, but for me it is almost always olfactory related. I close my eyes and lose myself in the intangible realm of my distant past . . .

Oh, wait. I've done it again.

This is harder than I thought. Here I am talking about trivial things like cigars, Windsor knots, and faces reminiscent of distressed leather . . . Meanwhile, you are probably wondering what, exactly, my story is about.

I think it would be best if I attempted to recount my story from the beginning, avoiding tangents wherever possible. I make no promises though, I am no novelist.

A Future Decided

I received an email at my terminal today. It read:

Cassandra Delaney <c.Delaney@DLE.gov.oc>
To: Alan Febras <a.febras@C36AB84T10184.ptn.oc
09:13am Tuesday 02-08-2051

Mr. Febras,
Congratulations on your upcoming 65th Birthday! Well done on making it this far. Pursuant to the Life Extension Act of 2048, an appointment has been made for your complete synthetic upgrade on the 13th of August 2051 at 9am.

Please make the effort to arrive for your appointment at the specified time, as it is considered an unlawful act to avoid this mandatory procedure. A penalty of Cr900 will be charged to your personal credit account for every 24 hour period you are missing. This is to compensate the Department of Life Extension for resources lost in locating and recovering you. A Cr250 delivery fee will also be charged when you are found on top of the existing penalty rate.

This is an exciting time for you, Mr. Febras. Your synthetic upgrade will allow you to fully integrate yourself into Oceana's exciting solar exploration and colonization programs. Step out of retirement, and see the Universe with your own newly improved eyes!

Please direct any questions you may have to the information terminal at: info@DLE.gov.oc

Have a safe day.
C. Delaney
Department of Life Extension, Oceana.

I read through the email a couple of times, barely absorbing the information at all. I knew this letter was coming, and I tell myself I shouldn't be this perturbed, yet I cannot seem to get my trembling digits to behave symbiotically with this mental announcement. They simply refuse to be rational, it seems. I turn my personal terminal screen off and figure I can put this out of my mind as I make some breakfast.

Of course, pressing a few buttons on the Ease-O-Meal 2.0 isn't exactly taxing or thought-engrossing enough to distract me by any detectable level. Twenty years of living with these matter assembly devices has not lessened my amazement of the far reaching scope of current technologies.

Most of us remember the commencement of what history calls "The Singularity", when a computer as smart as a human mind was thrust upon the world in 2018. Said computer began upgrading itself, providing us with the necessary technological blueprints to keep pace with its own vastly growing prowess. I don't know an excessive amount about it, but suffice to say we had all the scientific answers we wanted, and more that we didn't ask for as an added bonus. Even with humanity's seemingly built-in resistance to rapid change, rapidly change things did.

Bio-technology, Nano-technology, Eco-technology and lots of other fancy Prefix-technologies were readily available and slowly worming their way into everyday life. Yet somehow, despite the fact that a resource based economy was then distinctly possible, the monetary system remained, slowly taking the now modern form of digital credit. Scarcity was wiped out, but we still paid for things regardless. That did always confuse me. I guess *some* things will never change. Greed for instance.

The invading smell of perfectly cooked bacon and eggs tugs at my olfactory orifice and draws me away from my musings. I look down and the predictably flawless meal looks innocently back at me.

No pigs were harmed in the making of this meal, I joke to myself. It's all synthetic. Waste matter from my apartment is stored then converted at a molecular level to foodstuff at a push of a button. I remember the first prototypes were designed to simply convert the surrounding air, but suffocation was an unfortunate side effect for anyone standing ready to receive a meal.

As I bring my composite plastic cutlery down to begin my breakfast, I feel that ever recurring pang of desire to hold real steel in my hands again. The gentle weight and solid feel of metal is certainly not matched by the modern alternative. The yolk is soft, and bursts satisfyingly at the first prod. I notice yet again that the yellow is too bright, looking somewhat like an acrylic artist's paint I used to use in High School. Princess Yellow I believe it was called. I shrug apathetically, acceding to the demands of a hungry stomach, spearing some food and taking my first bite.

I hear a lot of people my age who ate *real* food complain that this stuff is not as good, but I am not so sure. It is identical even at a sub-atomic level to the food it is emulating. Perhaps we simply do not agree with the machine's view of a perfectly cooked meal. Maybe we like bacon a bit overdone? Eggs a bit rubbery? Toast slightly burnt and the butter more readily applied?

I personally miss the feeling of skill and accomplishment that came from perfecting a favorite recipe. I miss the stifling, humid summer kitchen and the sizzling contraction of raw meat as it touches down on a simmering pan. Of course, for all the ex-cooks that crave the old kitchen rituals, there are perhaps more of those who enjoy the fact that they don't have to sit through another burnt chop or watery soup. No longer do they risk having to run a red finger under cold water to soothe their clumsy mistakes.

Life certainly is safe, and an applicable alternative to that word is boring. Life certainly is boring these days. I often wonder if the element of danger in everyday living was what made life that much more interesting when I was younger. Things like driving a car, cooking over an open fire, playing any early 21st century sport and shaving with an actual blade. It didn't seem like much then, but you would get in some hot water if you attempted anything like that in 2051.

For your own good, of course.

I scrape the last remains of my calculably perfect breakfast up and finish slowly, still musing like I do most mornings. Well, I did successfully manage to put my upcoming appointment out of my mind for at least a small amount of time, which is a pleasant surprise. I dump my plate and cutlery in the waste storage vessel in the kitchen. It is cheaper to break down and reproduce plates than it is to clean them apparently. I never got that either. Yet it's easy, so no complaints there.

Luckily, the same cannot be said for cleaning humans, and I proceed to the washroom. This is even easier than breakfast, because eating still requires movement to some extent. Here, I just stand in what I can only call a pod, close the door and wait until the wash program has finished. No primitive nakedness and soap required. In fact, washing is more like a daily Nanobot checkup, complete with bright lights and authoritative bleeps. You get scanned, and any anomalies found are then eradicated. This includes any foreign bodies like dirt and bacteria, as well as internal infections and diseases.

Throw in your personal preference for grooming such as hair length and whether or not you want to keep that seedy-looking beard someone convinced you to grow out, and all your bathroom bases are covered.

You always walk away from a "wash" feeling very self-assured but not really clean in the traditional sense of the word, even though you are technically spotless. I guess the feeling of refreshment is missing somehow. Heaven forefend if someone wished to waste water on a traditional bathroom visit. Even if they somehow managed to find an abandoned bath and cake of soap, they would never get away with such an act of environmental disregard.

I attempt to avoid a glance into the convenient, albeit useless mirror on the bathroom wall. What are you meant to do with a mirror? Everything has already been fixed up in that claustrophobic and unusual pod. All there is to do is visually absorb my lined, weary appearance. No thanks. Youthful vanity still surfaces unabated from the elusive recesses of my mind. The core of my personality surges fourth at what always seems to be the wrong moment. I still get overly excited by what is entirely the domain of those in their prime, but I have the feeling that most of us old guys do (secretly or forthrightly). I steal a secretive look as I saunter out of what people still call a bathroom, despite the obvious contrary nature of this term. Not bad for an old man really. Technology helps, I guess.

Time to face the day.

For me, this requires mental fortitude and a vigorous application of taxing restraint against the angst produced by an overwhelmingly boring retirement. While the collective masses of shelved spinsters and waning widowers are given the freedom leave their retirement complex at will, the requisite credits that go hand in hand with even small scale explorations are lacking. We are given free accommodation at the price of our personal freedom.

For the lesser minded, or even just those resigned to their fate; living out the interim period of biological death and synthetic resurrection is not a hard task. One can enjoy a walk in the holographic park lands on floor thirteen (complete with the gaseous, plastic smell of faux-forest mist). If that does not interest you, why not chat with your fellow vapid vagrants about such stimulating subjects like the current weather patterns or what you had for your previous meal?

Exciting!

I keep to myself mainly, wondering around and star-ing out windows. I often go to the library, which is little more than a collection of specialized terminals offer-ing digital versions of literary classics. I find the act of reading off a screen severely detracts from the overall experience that the simple combination of paper and printing-press once provided, but of course there is no alternative.

No alternative . . .

That seems a common phrase that bounces around angrily in my mind more often than not. Why is it that in this latest batch of societal reforms, only one avenue of advancement is pursued whilst all other alternatives get callously disregarded? What is the harm of paper and ink? It may be more expensive to produce than binary code on a flickering screen, but why did they get rid of all the old books? That would have cost more than it was worth in my view. Despite this, the modern version of a library is where I spend most of my time, escaping the dreary confines of a safe and sterile life in the ca-pable hands of Alexandre Dumas or George Macdonald Frasier.

I get the feeling that it will be harder than usual to lose myself in a fantastical work of pixelized fiction to-day. I am afraid that the queasy notion of my upcom-ing upgrade has a rather firm grasp on my attentions at present. It is not every day that you are faced with an upcoming mandatory execution and rebirth.

I shuffle out my room and try not to look startled as my door slides shut behind me with excessive force, banging loudly as it does so. No matter how many times I walk through this doorway, I never get used to such needlessly excitable automata. As I wend my way down the sterile white hallways, avoiding the gazes of terse staff and vacant patients alike, I decide to head for one of the sun rooms that are hardly ever occupied. I be-lieve that its dependable emptiness is due in some part to the fact that it constantly smells of curdled cream with a sprinkling of sulphur, but I put up with the noxious wafting so I can have some time to myself.

I sit in a sunny spot at a window overlooking the city with which I can no longer interact with, creatively named City Twenty Three. That is, to be concise: City Twenty Three of Six Hundred and Twelve, Southern Mainland, Oceana. They used to call it Adelaide, Australia, but that was when the world had separate nations and governments. Nothing has an identity anymore, it seems. Everything is so very drab.

A thought occurs to me, as can often happen when you have assumed a philosophical slouch whilst bathed in the glow of the morning sun. Why does the Department of Life Extension threaten us poor sods with a penalty fee for not complying, when we have no Credits as a general rule? How is a debited account going to help them find us if we have decided to attempt a disappearing act? What absolute nonsense. I suppose it has something to do with swindling some other governmental department of their Credits through some bloated clause or insurance loophole. How do you track Credits anyway? It's certainly beyond me.

I am not sure if I am entirely comfortable with the idea of such a controlling and openly exacerbating government controlling my every step for potentially hundreds of extra years. I am torn between the obvious desire for self preservation and the very real disdain I have developed for the world around me. I see through their thinly veiled propaganda. My new life will likely be nothing more than a laborer on a colonization mission to who knows where. Haven't I spent enough of my life in servitude to others? Why should I simply extend that misery?

Of course, we could get to a new planet, mutiny and take to the stars as daring space pirates, legions of mutton dressed as electronic lambs laughing maniacally with the profound joy of a snatched freedom. The likelihood of that happening outside my fantasies is not very high, I'd imagine.

I don't want to die just yet. Sixty-five is really not that old, especially with the level of technology available to fix us up at the drop of a hat. I guess it comes down to what is cheaper; constantly fixing a dying organic machine, or replacing it with a lower maintenance synthetic one? Upgraded humans reportedly eat less, sleep less, breathe less (the lungs convert inhaled particles into stored energy), and are a far more efficient version of the original. No human at sixty can be used for intensive labor jobs, even on our own planet. The newer version is simply a better design. Natural selection has been replaced with digital optimization. Evolution is now firmly in our hands.

What about reproduction? Synthesized. I am sure they will simplify and optimize that too, so that no unseemly friction and gyration will be needed in the not-too-distant future. Sounds thrilling.

I pass the morning in solitude sprinkled with a pinch of despair. I keep fighting off the anger that flares up when I realize I should be doing something with my last days on earth in my natural-born body, that I should satiate my soul before it is digitized or destroyed. I then must consequently endeavor to lift my spirits from a rather rapid slump as it dawns on me yet again that I have nobody left to share these moments with anyway.

James, my last true friend and companion was upgraded a few months ago. I have not seen him again, as expected. He is probably on a ship to some ghastly planet and working hours upon hours to appease some mad political desire to spread mechanized humanity throughout the stars. The thought drives me to the depths of despair. He was such a free thinker, such an optimist. He always had some new madcap plan that enveloped him entirety, each drastically different from the last. James was very political, but took surprisingly well to the concept of an upgrade. He seemed to think that it would enhance his capacity to reason.

Listen to me, would you? I make it sound like he is dead.

My beloved and cherished wife died some twenty years back, an agonizing, soul-shattering moment. I have not being complete since that day. The tragic consequences of random luck bear down on me more than I should let it, but I cannot escape the fury against such injustice even after a few decades of reflection. The pain still burns as if new and raw on some days. So, yes; I am absolutely alone. This prompts me more often than not to question why I am so determined to keep on living through life extension.

My guess is fear.

Look, I don't think I want to bore you anymore with the dreary nature of my day to day life. Honestly, there is not much more to say about it other than it is lonely, boring and requires no attention whatsoever. Even manually cooking my own dinner would entertain me these days.

I close my eyes and let the morning slowly drift by without me.

"Alan bloody Febras!" a hearty voice booms from behind me. "Are you going to sit there all day?"

I look around and a jarring smile sears across my saggy features unbidden, bringing animation and life to a previously placid face.

"James!" I croak. "I was just thinking about you."

A Tangent Apparition

"So what's it like?"

"Hard to describe, Alan," muses James, his gaze anchored to my ambient fireplace as if he has no idea the flames are entirely holographic. Green and orange light pulses sporadically upon the stark white walls, lending some personality to a staid abode.

I notice how imposing he looks in the dim light. Large, brown eyebrows dominate a square face, with his deep-set grey eyes regarding the sparse furniture in barely concealed disdain. His frame looks rather lithe and imposing, but I cannot imagine the government creating obese synthetic constructs.

We had hastily crept back to my tiny apartment as soon as I managed to overcome the sudden raw and heady shock of seeing him again. He was seemingly uncaring of the legal considerations that arose from his unscheduled appearance at a biologically inhabited zone. I was concerned enough for the both of us however, and whisked him out of sight as soon as I regained the capacity to form a coherent sentence.

"Do you feel different, I mean."

"Not in any obvious way, I generally feel strong, healthy and quite content with my new body's stamina and prowess. These are my thoughts in my head, and it really just feels like I woke up from surgery in a body of a twenty-five year old athlete."

I look at him in contemplation. James has a bad habit of glossing over any unpleasantries while simultaneously exaggerating all the good points. His stories always have to be good ones, even if truth is often treated like an unwelcome guest to be ignored as tactfully as possible.

"Is it still you, James?" I press on. "Can you honestly tell me that you feel this is a continuation of yourself, instead of a re-invention?"

He looks at me with an expression of surprised curiosity, as if he hasn't had anyone ask him a meaningful question for some time. His thin lips form a smile. I attempt my best casually indifferent expression in response, but the shock of looking at a young version of your oldest friend is surreal to put it mildly. Add in the aspect of synthesis, and it cannot be denied my mind is swimming in some bizarre and uncharted waters.

James leans back slowly on what can only be called a utilitarian chair. Comfort is not big in transitional facilities; function is unashamedly predominate.

"No," he states flatly. "I can tell you want the truth from me Alan, despite your feigned casual approach."

He gets the desired reaction from me as I let out a saddened gasp. I see his expression soften as the realization of my upcoming upgrade surfaces in his mind. Yet he continues his explanation unabated.

"The man I once was is dead in more than just a physical manner, Alan. I feel like a copy of the original, but I didn't believe such at first and I am sure that some do not to this day. There is simply something . . . missing. I still feel emotions perfectly. Quite often sadness of late, truth be told, at the discovery of the parody that I inhibit."

"I don't understand."

"Think of it this way, old friend," James says in a conversational tone. "On a quiet night, when there is nothing but me and my thoughts, I notice a deep and profound stillness in the back of my mind. It is as if a tiny speck is steadily seeping an inky blackness, a darkness that draws in the spark of my synapses like a black hole. It is a lack of something that I cannot fully describe, but is the more profound because of its subtlety."

"Your soul?"

"I guess you could call it that, in a manner of speaking. Whatever force kept me alive has ceased to be, and

I am a mere representation of the person that has gone. Perfectly executed, but not alive in a traditional sense. I wouldn't call it the soul so much as the spark of life."

His explanation stops just as suddenly as it started. I see tears forming, and I am struck at how odd it is that tears were carried over from the original human blueprint.

"It is odd, Alan, to mourn your own death. I will hopefully get used to this new me, and perhaps it is better living this way that simply ceasing to be, but I am really not certain. While a lot of people may be fooled, I am not."

"I am so sorry James," I whisper from a numbed face. "You make me dread my upgrade even more that I already was."

His eyes snap into focus and bore directly into mine. I see a sharp glint of intent surface in his sober expression. He rapidly looks around the room as if to gather his thoughts, and then regards me once more.

"Don't worry about me Alan. I am learning to live with my new . . . life." He stops purposefully, and narrows his eyes in scrutiny. "What did you say just then about dreading your upgrade?"

"Nothing really James, I was merely sharing the fear I have of my obligatory appointment that is rapidly approaching. I am sure a lot of people go through it."

"Most people rather look forward to a shot at immortality Alan. Do you not share this desire?"

I am caught off guard, as just previously James had been outlining is sorrow and confusion regarding his synthesis. I look at him in an obvious state of confusion, and he gives a hearty laugh at my apparent distress. It is my turn to lean back on the unyielding surface of my chair.

"Forgive my crass approach to this subject Alan, please do," he says, "I would like to know more of your thoughts regarding this impending upgrade."

"I don't see the point mate," I state, slightly put off by his demeanor. "It really doesn't matter if I am totally sold on the idea or not, because I am not ready to die just yet."

James slowly nods, a smile dancing on his lips. "Just indulge me, dear friend, please do."

I sigh. At least his personality is exactly preserved, if not his mysterious spark of life.

I begin testily, "I really wish there was another option. Maybe I would be content with death if I lived another decade or two? So what if my mind is a bit muddled by then, and they cannot upgrade me? This lack of freedom concerning my own fate is saddening and infuriating at the same time. I just want to be given some choices."

"Indeed?" he responds. "Choices make our paths divergent Alan, that much is true."

"It's a moot point James."

A silence descends between us. I try and appear relaxed but we can both sense my growing discontent. Talking so nonchalantly about my approaching physical doom is certainly not going to brighten my mood in any way. This welcome intrusion into my day is fast decaying into an overtly divergent and deathly discourse.

"What if I could give you another way out?" he asks eventually in a soothing tone. "An extension of your mortal coil that does not require the mechanization of your soul? Such is the true purpose of my visit to you, old friend."

"What are you saying?" My heart palpitates with sudden excitement. "What kind of scheme are you cooking up this time James?"

He laughs. "You will be pleased to learn that it is not my scheme at all, Alan. I am merely the messenger and courier to a new life."

"Please, James," I plead "Can you dispense with the poetic spin? Just tell me of your so-called opportunity so that I may calm down and think clearly again?"

He leans forward, slightly disappointed at being deprived of a chance to flamboyantly deliver his well practiced speech. "Okay, okay Alan. You admittedly take the fun out of life or death situations sometimes."

Even I can manage a small chuckle at this.

James continues, "My very smart friend has been developing a monumental piece of technology. He has spent his lifetime dedicated unwaveringly to one field of research, and this has culminated into something incredible." He pauses to give me an excited grin, clasping his hands together tightly as if to restrain himself. "Nothing short of amazing, Alan, and that's an understatement."

"You stall, James," I interject tersely, trying to condense his sales pitch down to bare facts.

"Not at all, I simply need to emphasize the genius of what I am about to tell you so you can more easily soak it in."

I nod slowly, realizing I will not escape an embellished narrative this time around.

"I have to tell you, even though I gather you have already surmised it, that this person operates most definitely outside the staid constraints of law. It speaks volumes of his talent that he has never been discovered, and yet he lives only a few blocks from this very complex."

"That is . . . actually quite impressive." He has my attention now.

"Indeed. Now brace yourself Alan. You must agree that the scope and reach of current technology far surpasses even our wildest speculations of youth?"

"Absolutely."

"Would it be such a stretch then, to imagine that what can effectively be called time travel has been developed?"

I stare in bewilderment, feeling rather disappointed that this obvious fiction is the catalyst of his announcement. "Yes . . . that would still be a stretch for me James."

"If I am to speak in a forthright manner, the device has very limited capacity," he continues unperturbed, still leaning forward in a hunched conspirator's pose. "You may only go back and re-inhabit your old mind, to simplify the science."

"So you mean I extend my life by re-living it?" I ask in a disappointed tone. "That sounds a bit repetitious to say the least."

"Not at all, Alan. Like I stated before, I cannot explain the science. I will leave that to my learned friend if you decide to meet him. Suffice to say that the multiple universe theory from the long forgotten Quantum Mechanics theorem has been proven to be correct. As soon as your mind travels back to your old body, you will have split into a previously identical, but separate reality."

"I don't really understand."

"It would be your life exactly as you lived it up until the moment you arrive within yourself," James clarifies patiently. "From then nothing is set in stone, for you will inhabit a divergent universe. It would be a new life, as even if you wanted to make the same life-journey back to the present, more than likely the present will not be the same the second time around. It may be close, or it may be astronomically different. Think of the possibilities Alan!"

My mind is reeling under the relenting barrage of renewed hope and excitement in what was a broken life. I ask in a shaky voice, "Would I be able to upgrade at the end of my second life?"

"You aren't quite grasping this Alan!" James grins slightly. "There may not even be a Singularity this second time around. It may happen hundreds of years later, or not at all. This is a new realm of opportunity."

I pause reflectively, and I find myself starting to begrudgingly accept his fantastical assertions as truth. "I . . . think I am beginning to grasp the general premise of this technology. But how in blazes do you know it works?"

"Well, since you are sending someone into an alternate reality, there is no way that can simply contact you in fifty years time and announce its success. There are ways, however, to verify the initial process has been successful." He hesitates for a moment, weighing his words carefully. "This is not my area of expertise, but imagine throwing a bowling ball into the ocean. You can certainly verify that it has left your hands, and you can see it breaking the surface of the water, but after that you will likely never see it again. You can still assume it hasn't randomly disappeared however."

"Why is that such an easy assumption to make?" I ask angrily, trying to hide the incredulous tone that has crept into my voice.

"Because energy does not simply disperse, even between universes. It travels and morphs. It is constant. The unbelievable nature of this technology is the transfer of energy between the two separate universes, without disrupting the balance to a negative effect."

"This sounds like Russian-Roulette." My voice is laced with doubt.

"That's because I am butchering the beauty of this marvelous technology with my clumsy words and plodding explanations."

I make a noncommittal grunt.

"It is either synthetic rebirth or an organic life extension to choose between Alan. I know death is not an option for you at this point."

I look to my feet. What James is trying to tell me sounds like sheer fantasy. Then again, so does a lot of current technology when reflecting on what life used to offer. What scares me is the prospect of showing up at a mad scientist's secret lair and being used as an unwilling test subject. My trust in my oldest friend and the lack of any other choice compels me to at least consider what is being offered. The slightest possibility of suddenly being in the prime of my life again instead of this weakened body seems worth the risk of sudden oblivion. After all, I am going to my death in a way soon enough, only to be reborn as a functioning memoriam of my own mind. I think that disturbs me more that I would care to admit.

"I am terribly sorry to rush you Alan, but this offer is one time only." He is looking intently at me. "It is understandably risky for me to be in a designated biological area, and although I will admit securely guarding old men is not on this government's top priority list, the chance of being discovered does increase dramatically in public spaces."

"I understand," I say quietly. "But I do have one final question."

"Of course."

"What does this man ask of me in return for a new life?" I dread the response. "Surely there is some catch."

"None," states James simply. "He is a Libertarian, quite frankly, and he believes he is offering the last chance of freedom to any who would be brave enough to claim it. He needs spokesmen like me to gather any willing souls, as his own compromise will destroy any further opportunity to set humanity free."

"How long have you known this person?"

"Long enough Alan, there is a lot about my past you never knew."

I sense the time to decide soon approaches, and sweat gathers on my brow in anticipatory fear. In a life of no real choices comes the sudden apparition of a monumental tangent dancing enticingly within a fleeting window of opportunity. It causes a huge strain in my mind which was until this day, placid and bored.

"You do realize the immensity of what you ask James?" I stammer. "You give me no time to think this over."

"Time dilutes the purity of your thoughts," he retorts acid-tongued. "Given leave for contemplation you will always select the easiest and safest choice. The option you know the most about provides more facts to twist and contort in order to arrive at a desirous conclusion. Yet you are simply giving into fear."

"What are you trying to say?" I ask wearily, not at all motivated at the prospect of verbally sparring with him and his sneering morality.

"You probably regard fear as a chilling and potent enemy, but in reality it is a friend. A safety blanket. A ready excuse to fall back on when you breach your comfort zone. When you can recognize your fear as a serpentine confidant rather than a brooding enemy, making hard choices will become easier. Only the crux of pressure can force a pure outlook out of a heavy burden."

My shoulders sag.

Something in his harsh speech resonates with me. I find truth in the prospect of my choosing the safest option, given the time to mull it over. It is something I have always done, yet I strongly believe I am not alone in this fallacy.

So here I sit, outwardly silent with a maelstrom of emotions thrashing around beneath the surface. This is seemingly my wish come true; a chance to live my life again, free from horrid restrictions and the suffocating weight of banality. To be transported back to the last era of freedom, to sample once more all the luxuries of my memory and explore a range of new possibilities. To see the smile of my beloved wife again, to feel her warmth.

All I risk is my life.

A thought blooms from the darkest recesses of my mind that I am guaranteed death in under a month. Sure, I may live on in technicality, but what if I am one of the unlucky ones who feels their own death as potently as the man sitting across from me? A pathetic living-parody of myself, entirely aware of the devolved state of my own mind. That is beginning to seem the more harrowing choice to take.

"You already knew what my decision would be, didn't you James?"

"I believe so, yes," he says in a quietly confident tone. "You're a smart guy Alan."

I stand up, body shaking with the sort of surging adrenaline that I thought myself incapable of feeling anymore. I look around the white room with the triumphant feeling of one who is escaping a prison cell. "No point hanging around this charnel house then James."

"Agreed."

Journey

The humming overhead light is invasively bright.

I am, for lack of a better phrase, lying sandwiched between bulky metallic parts on a thin padded table, under which are more abnormally large mechanical components. A series of tubes and wires connect one machine-hub to another, but certainly not in a discernable pattern. I have been strapped in rather tightly. Groans of leather remind me that sitting up would be an unachievable aim at present.

The gentle, pulsing electronic tones of surrounding machinery helps to soothe my nervous disposition. This snatched calmness, however, is slowly countered by the glaring sheen of highly polished metal agitating my vision, forcing me to squint. A voice cuts through the ambience and my eyes search for the speaker.

"Alan, we are almost set," states Mr. Montgomery in a quiet and assured manner. "Just remember what we have talked about regarding this procedure. Think of this device as a rather large photo camera. Your body will not be physically harmed during the procedure, and should one attempt fail, we will simply start over with no harm done whatsoever."

"What happens if it works?' I ask. "To my body, I mean."

"Success in the procedure is indicated by a complete lack of higher brain function, as your consciousness will no longer be attached to your mind so to speak. At least not in this timeline." He lets out a soft laugh. Slightly off-putting . . .

"I see . . ."

"We then disintegrate your remains."

"Uhhh . . .."

"Not to worry, Mr. Febras, not to worry at all. By that time you will be back in your previous self living a new, wonderful life of possibility and freedom."

"Sounds fine," I say half-heartedly, almost wishing he would stop stalling. Almost . . .

"Friends too, dear old friends . . ." I nod politely as I watch him slip into a deep reverie.

"No need for the sales-pitch now, Mr. Montgomery," I say a bit too loudly, wrenching out my best gentlemanly facade as he slowly turns to regard me.

"Of course!" He chuckles softly, seeming not to notice how long he had delayed by daydreaming. "I shall be back momentarily and we can begin."

It has been a good couple of hours since I arrived at this quirky mix of antique showroom and high-tech laboratory (I cannot for the life of me figure out which is more illegal). Most of that time has been spent in discussion with the amazingly gifted man whom has just left the workshop. I couldn't repeat a quarter of the explanation given to me as to why this whole concept is a sound one, but I was convinced enough to get strapped into this "giant camera" so that is that. Not to say that I am not in an absolute panic regarding the success of such a bizarre undertaking.

As eloquently as Mr. Montgomery explained his theory, I still don't really get it.

Something about his dedication to his ideals impresses me though, so much more than apathetic governmental employees forcing their solution down your throat ever could. It really is beyond the point of no return now, but that was on the cards back at the transitional facility anyway. I think I prefer the unknown now I am committed to it fully.

"How I wish I had the opportunity that you do Alan . . ." announces the sudden and unexpected voice of James in a saddened tone. "I missed this boat by just a few weeks. I begged Mr. Montgomery to let me be the first, but he said I was too important to experiment on."

"Am I the first?" I blurt in hurried panic, trying to turn my head and meet his synthetic gaze.

"No, I would never do that to you Alan. I have seen this work hundreds of times now."

"Umm . . . where are you?"

"I am in the observation booth mate; I am talking to you via some speakers in the room."

"Oh."

"Nervous?"

"Shitting myself."

He laughs solemnly. "At least we are disintegrating your body afterwards, so I don't have to clean that mess up."

"Very nice." I smile.

"Would you like some music to soothe the nerves?" His voice distorts slightly though the speakers.

"I doubt that will help much, but sure."

The room is instantly flooded with the sublime sounds of Vivaldi's La Tempesta di Mare. I laugh out loud. Soothe the nerves indeed. James couldn't have picked a more rousing and personal piece of music if he tried. Adrenaline surges unabated as the movement reaches its first crescendo, and I cannot help but feeling this is an apt sound-track for the epic journey I will shortly be taking.

"Better?" I can practically hear James' grin over the speakers.

"You haven't changed that much James, if you can still be this much of a pain."

"Pain?" says a second voice from within the room, and I notice Mr. Montgomery regarding me with an almost offended expression. "Surely you cannot call such a piece painful Mr. Febras?"

"I . . . no . . ." I stammer in surprise. "James was feigning concern in relaxing me when he selected this of all music to play."

Mr. Montgomery lets out a sharp laugh and pats me gently on the shoulder. "I understand Alan, of course. Very funny James."

"Thank you," he responds mirthfully.

"Now," Mr. Montgomery says, his features losing all trace of amusement. "I have to warn you that this procedure involves a lot of intense pain staggered in short intervals. I cannot medicate you, for that may interfere with the integrity of the data I can get from your mind."

Well, that was a change of pace . . . I think to myself.

"We can begin as soon as you are ready."

My heart starts to race. The surge of adrenaline I feel at these words in astounding. This is absolutely the most afraid I have been in my life. It is a strange situation indeed when one is in charge of beckoning the commencement of an event that will most certainly change their life in a devastatingly effective way. Death may become of such a powerful verbal ushering. I can feel the seconds drag by as if weighed down by the universe itself. It feels as if my entire existence has been leading to this singular moment in time. Tears begin to gather of their own volition, as the sheer emotive state slowly renders my mind catatonic. Before I let my fear overcome me entirely, I force out the single most important word I have ever spoken in my life:

"Go."

Bright, searing pain invades every fiber of my being; agony I cannot believe the human body is capable of experiencing. I am unaware that I am screaming until the sensation passes, and before I stop the dreadful experience begins anew. I lose my awareness of anything but the singular paroxysm tormenting every last nerve.

A terrible rhythm emerges as the suffering stops just before I can pass out in overwhelmed agony, then starts anew right before I can regain focus. I try and force my eyes open, but am greeted with burning white light that stings like a thousand suns. Somehow I can momentarily hear the leather restraints straining under my thrashing limbs before I lose concentration once more. Vivaldi reaches my ear in broken fragments between convulsions. There is no possible way I can continue enduring this torture.

I feel an unnatural heat permeate somewhere around me, and it sounds like my screams have gotten louder.

Then silence.

I can no longer feel my body.

Thin rivulets of purple and crimson sparks slither in a liquid dance around me as pulsating grey clouds of viscous matter seep ribbons of velvet blue.

I am disembodied. Time is now, and not at all. Here is nowhere and everywhere all at once. Whatever I am transformed unto floats here, barely held together with sharp cords of golden light. Arching tones of shrill treble permeate the rippling liquid skies above me, tracing obscure patterns that I cannot follow with my meager makeshift sight.

With sudden terror, I feel a suffocating grip surround me. It engulfs me slowly, holding me with tangled tendrils. It pulls me down, slowly at first then with ever gaining momentum. My surroundings blur in a chaotic swirling pattern as I pass them in increasing speed. Soon I cannot see anything but pale orange mist melting away as I sear past at a blinding pace.

Crackling bolts of energy begin to surround me, becoming more numerous the faster I descend. One by one they enter my disembodied soul and writhe in electric symphony. I begin to feel infused with a strange energy as they grow in number.

A deep pulsating tremor reaches out from either side of me and grows in volume and rapidity. From below me I hear the loud elemental wail of reality torn asunder. White-hot oceans of liquid heat cascade from the breach like a volcanic eruption, yet still I descend ever faster.

As I get pulled into the furiously spitting maw of this newly formed chasm, I find that the surrounding heat is barely warm as I enter its voluminous embrace. I journey downwards still, getting strangely colder the further

I descend. The colors that surround me gradually fade from a searingly bright yellow to a muted grey tone the deeper I go. I begin to notice more resistance from my environment in letting me pass.

It is as if the liquidity of my surrounds is slowly diminishing, like I am being pulled into concrete that is beginning to set.

The stony-grey tomb that encompasses me grows darker as it slowly hardens. My approach slows significantly in the wake of such heavy friction.

Eventually, I stop.

My disembodied presence is somehow held firm in these dark confines. A tingling sensation emits from somewhere nearby and I realize with amazement that I can feel my fingers moving against the unforgiving solidity of this claustrophobic sepulcher. With this revelation in mind, I begin focusing on rediscovering my other limbs. Time drags by as feeling slowly returns to my body. Confusion reigns absolute as I try and discover just where I am. Suddenly, I feel the strong urge to breathe. This is bad, as I cannot seem to move at all within this unyielding edifice.

Panic rises quickly, and I can actually feel my heart begin to race once more. I will celebrate the return of said sensation later, as the realization that I am slowly suffocating has taken precedent in my mental itinerary. As well it should.

Muscles strain uselessly against solid matter as I try and break free of what feels like an immitigable prison. I feel a scream of primal fury well up from deep inside me. From the depths of my body, I let lose a magnificent roar. I yell unceasingly until my ears ring out in protest. I feel my life slipping away scream by blood-curdling scream.

My eyes snap open.

Awakening

The sound of steady, rhythmic breathing next to me confuses me greatly.

I blink my eyes rapidly, attempting to gain focus, and then realize with profound joy that I can move my body freely. I am swathed from head to toe in sweat, laying down on an exceedingly comfortable (albeit soaked) mattress. My head snaps to the side in bewilderment as my eyes search for the person making beautifully contented sleeping noises. I cry out with shock and she awakens groggily.

"Alan . . . what's wrong honey?" she yawns. "Did you have a nightmare?"

My eyes widen in panic as I sit upright in on the bed, shaking violently. I breathe heavily as my eyes dart around the darkened room searching for answers.

"Wow," the woman exclaims, becoming more awakened at the sight of such obtuse behavior. She turns the bedside lamp on, bathing the room in a yellow glow. "You are absolutely covered in sweat. I've never seen you like this . . . Are you ok sweetie?"

I turn to look at her, and feel my heart melt away in the fire of ecstatic revelation.

Audrey.

My gorgeous wife is lying right here next to me, naked and worried and I don't understand how. I look down at my own body and draw a sharp intake of breath.

Impossible. I think to myself automatically in the characteristic denial borne of an unfathomable circumstance.

In the place of a withered old man is a young man in his prime.

Me.

I am . . . inhabiting my previous self. I feel overcome with a heady mix of happiness and displacement.

"I . . . had a really bad nightmare," I stammer as I turn back to her. My goodness, she is more perfect than I remember her. Alabaster skin and long auburn hair with the most piercing green eyes I have ever encountered. Her face is gentle and welcoming, even in the dead of night, and her full lips are pouted in concern. Audrey catches my eyes taking in the splendid sight of her naked body and she gives a confused laugh.

"You act like you have not seen a naked woman in some time." She arches her back purposefully, showing off her full chest and giggles sleepily. "That must have been a pretty potent nightmare."

"It went on for a lifetime," I reply in a dazed tone. I notice how smooth and youthful my voice sounds compared what I am used to hearing.

Audrey looks at me with renewed concern. "Are you sure you are alright love? You look like shit."

I laugh heartily at such playful swearing. I had forgotten how easy-going the world used to be. "I'm ok, just a bit shaken."

"Alright love, I'm going back to sleep then."

"Audrey . . . wait."

She glances back with genuine worry etched in her features. "What's wrong sweetie?"

"I . . . love you so, so much." I feel tears of joy stream down my face in rivulets of pure, distilled emotion. I can hear the primal tones of halting breath slowly breach my tightly clenched teeth.

"Come here you crazy cat." She holds her arms out and tries to not to look too disquieted with my erratic decorum. What a sweetheart. "You need big cuddles."

I gladly accede and lay in her arms, bathed in a glow of heady contentment and listening to her steady heartbeat with something akin to rapture. We are together again, in the most unbelievable of scenarios. I am here; effectively back in time, ready to live life all over again. Escaping enslavement and gaining freedom. Most importantly; I am back in my lover's warm, soft embrace.

I hug Audrey tightly, as if making sure she is still there. My beloved stirs, as if she was just dropping off to sleep again.

"Should I turn off the light sweetie?" she says dreamily. "You want to try and sleep again?"

"Not really . . ." I respond hesitatingly. "I was hoping you could help me take my mind off that nightmare."

Audrey laughs tiredly. "You are a devil Alan Febras. It's three in the morning."

I lean down and kiss her, bridging the gap of twenty years in a sublime and lasting moment. All my sorrow transforms into renewed passion and pertinacious bliss the instant our lips touch.

"You make a persuasive argument," she purrs contentedly. "I guess we can leave the light on for another hour."

That night I slept more soundly than I have in twenty years.

***

When I awoke that morning, I was half expecting to be staring at the white walls of my apartment in the transitional centre, a victim of a lucid dream of monumental proportions. I was exhilarated to be proven wrong. The ripple-iron ceiling of our Nineteenth century cottage greeted me with all its quirky imperfections. I cannot express the sheer delectation derived from viewing the simple sight of an old ceiling in my waking moments.

My nostrils flare as I take a slow, luxuriant breath. There is an intoxicating aroma of musty humanity about the room. The sweet, pungent scent of stale sweat and sexually soiled linen mixes with the crisp, acrid coolness of an autumn morning. It is so beautifully hedonistic in its salacious and unpretentious way. A far cry from the sterile and indurate awakening experienced not one morning ago.

I stretch slowly, determined to soak in every last sensation provided from what would be considered frivolous and opulent furnishings where I came from. Audrey shudders slightly under the feather-light touch of my fingertips as I trace the contours of her still sleeping body. The realization that I am back in my prime, that the far flung promise of James has actually come true warms my body in a soothing engulfment.

Taking care not to disturb the beautifully serene Audrey, I slide out of bed and reach for the fluffy and inviting black bathrobe hanging from a screw on the door. As I drape it over my cold shoulders, I am struck with the supreme comfort attained from such a simple article of clothing. I open the door as quietly as possible and begin my exploration of my past made manifest.

The narrow hallway of my old cottage greets me in the dim morning light. I make my way to the living room and glance at the calendar. It is the first of April, 2012. April Fool's day. I laugh out loud, musing at the coincidence of such a day to return to my old life. Still chuckling, I shuffle sleepily to the kitchen and take in the wonderfully ordered chaos of a well used room. Last night's dishes are stacked neatly, complete with crumbs and dirty cutlery on top. We couldn't be bothered washing the dishes that night, I note with surprising glee. Even a small mess like this is alien and new to one who has lived so forcibly neat for years.

Excitement washes over me anew at the prospect of having the opportunity to cook for myself again. I take stock of what we have in the fridge and cupboards, taking my time to rediscover the cluttered collection of treats and staples that were part of everyday life. I notice a small brass Ibrik sitting by the stove-top. At first I am puzzled as to the diminutive nature of the coffee pot, but I soon remember how much Audrey loathes coffee. I smile, and wonder if I still have the skill to brew some Turkish coffee.

An old morning ritual surfaces from the back of my mind as I relive the memory of my standing at this very stove, stirring eggs in a skillet over a low flame and watching the bubbling brew in the adjacent Ibrik out the corner of my eye.

I hasten to the fridge again to search for eggs. There they are, sitting proudly in their pulpy cardboard carton. *Awesome.*

I find a bowl to whisk them in and beat frantically, perhaps over zealously. I laugh giddily as I watch droplets of pale yellow mixture decorate the floorboards. I shrug my shoulders in apathy and ignore the mess.

The bowl makes a dull thud on the counter top as I set it down clumsily. I turn the stove on in childlike glee and watch as the potent blue flames of gas shoot up in a proud, primal display. Wooden spoon in hand, I place a well used pan down on the lit stove top and let it warm up.

A rich, earthy aroma gently massages my olfactories as I open a tin of finely ground Turkish coffee. I have decided to go all out and attempt to recreate the first remembered meal that popped into my head as I entered the kitchen, bridging memory and reality with each action I take. I notice I am still holding the wooden spoon, and exchange it for a more sensibly sized teaspoon with a wry smile. I know I used to like it strong, but I think even someone with a waxed tongue would turn down that dosage.

I fill the Ibrik with cool water and layer the coffee on top, taking care not to stir the grinds down, and then bring it over to join the now warmed fry-pan. This is all coming back so easily.

I cut small slithers of cooking butter from its paper packaging and ease them into the pan. Rich, creamy aromas waft from the pan as the butter slowly melts in a swirling display. I turn the adjacent element on as low as it can go and place the Ibrik over the barely perceptible flame.

Here we go.

The eggs sizzle gently as I pour them on the warmed surface of the pan. Immediately, I begin to stir, making sure not to let hard lumps form. As I begin the slow, relaxing process of cooking my first real breakfast, my mind is given a chance to wander.

Standing here, on these old polished floorboards in this quirky cottage kitchen seems bizarre and surreal. A soft morning breeze makes its way through some gaps in the window sill. I inhale deeply, noticing how the damp autumn air mixes with the fragrance of slowly brewing coffee and creamy eggs. I feel connected with the world in a way I have not in years. Everything seems more . . . tangible than I ever remember it being.

A loud, arresting hissing sound diverts my attention to the left of the simmering eggs, and I turn to behold dark brown foam bubbling over the sides of the Ibrik. Quickly, I yank the small brass pot off the stove and stir the remaining foam back down into the coffee.

Damn, I love the foam.

I take the pan off the heat for a moment to devote all of my attention to finishing my morning coffee. This time I watch closely as the potent brew foams steadily higher, and I take the pot off the stove just as it is about to spill over the rim. Perfect. I set it aside to let the grinds settle, and put the pan back on the heat to finish the eggs.

Almost done now, and without any major catastrophes. I put some bread in the toaster with a salivating mouth. This is going to be great.

"Eggs again?" asks a soft, sleepy voice from behind me. "You should consider Weet-Bix sometime dear, helps with digestion."

We laugh together in muted morning tones. "Just had a craving, love," I say sheepishly.

"Did you have withdrawals?" she jokes. "The shakes? Look at the mess you made."

"I do apologize," I say in a feigned stuffy tone, as I serve up my meal. "We really should not have fired the maid."

"A maid . . . I wish. That would be the day."

I sit down to my breakfast while she makes herself some tea and cereal. It tastes satisfyingly decadent, just how I remember it; soft, creamy and rich . . . but something is missing. Audrey regards me with a curious expression.

"You must be feeling odd today," she muses jokingly. "Where's the ever-present pepper on those eggs?"

Of course! It has been a long time since I have had the simple pleasure of shaking some spice over my meal. I search about the table for a pepper shaker, and my eyes settle on two bull horns with S and P carved into them.

Real horns . . . As spice vessels?

Every small forgotten detail engages my attention with a vice grip, and this is no exception. I gingerly grip the horn marked P and examine it with marvel.

"Your eggs are going cold Rain Man," Audrey teases.

"Oh . . . yeah," I mutter, and apply some finely ground pepper to my meal.

Delicious.

A gentle scraping sound announces Audrey pulling the chair out next to me. She plonks down unceremoniously, clutching her mug of tea and bowl of cereal. We eat in a contented silence for a while, before I notice her looking at the clock in a distracted way.

"What is it love?" I query.

"Not to be a buzz-kill honey, but didn't you say you had to be in early at work today?"

My heart sinks. Work. I may not remember the novel pepper shaker, but I do remember work. More distinctly, the loathing I felt for it. I worked (or should I now be saying work?) in upper level management for a governmental call centre. High pressure, good pay and a comfortable office chair. I recall just how much I hated going to work every day, but I was always too attached to the salary to take a risk finding a new job.

Not even the rich, velvety Turkish coffee can fully cheer me up as I sip it in reflection of Audrey's words. This is not exactly the welcome back party I was imagining this day would be. I find my years of wisdom already forming new notions of what will be important this second time around.

"Fuck it," I say flippantly. "I'll chuck a sickie."

A mischievous grin works its way into her features. "Sounds brilliant," she muses. "I've been trying to convince you to use up some of your sick leave for ages now. What an odd change of heart. Are you sure you are feeling normal?"

"Better than I have in a long time."

She sighs happily. "You won't hear any complaints from me .We don't get enough time together."

We finish sipping our drinks happily; giving each other silly smiles like naughty, truant children.

"What do you want to do with your secret-sickie?" she asks after a while.

"Absolutely nothing," I say. "Just have a nice day at home with you."

"Mmmm . . . Sounds gorgeous," she exclaims silkily. "I like this new attitude you have randomly adopted."

I lean in and kiss her softly. Never in my life had anyone been so understanding and supportive than my dearest Audrey. Being here with here now makes me realize just how much I missed her, and how lucky I was to find her in the first place. Most people settle down, never finding their perfect companion.

We are not most people.

Leaning back in the chair, I slowly take in my surroundings once more, examining more closely the relics of my fading memory turned corporeal. The table is scratched and rather worn. I remember us both agreeing not to bother re-varnishing it, as its unique personality would not survive the process of making it more presentable. I look up at the walls, where Audrey's beautiful, intricate artwork hangs proudly in expensive black frames. It took me a long time to convince her to display her delicate, soulful works so publicly, but I won the battle in the end, and our cottage is all the more perfect because of it. A quaint coffee mill sits next to a copper kettle, and next to that a tin of toffees. Nothing really seems to match with anything else in the room. Badly made mugs from a pottery lesson take pride of place on a shelf, right next to intricate Noritake Chinaware.

Beautiful chaos.

I take a final sip of my coffee, stopping just before I get a mouth full of thick sediment. I notice with some surprise Audrey is letting her tea go almost stone cold, and then it suddenly occurs to me that this was her usual habit. A strange disquiet comes over me as I wrestle with the notion that I am very close to being a stranger in my own life, such is the distance that time has brought. On the other hand, I find myself adapting with surprising ease to such a mind boggling situation. Life *is* how I remember it being, the struggle is in the act of remembrance itself, in rediscovering the little stitches that sew together the intricate tapestry of daily life.

It is like finding your favorite old coat in a forgotten drawer. It slips on comfortably like a second skin. After a few minutes happily swaggering around the bedroom, you casually slip your hand in your jacket pocket and pull out something strange like an old brass padlock. You don't remember putting that there, or even why, but there it is.

It's no big deal, I guess, as long as you don't pull out a mouse trap or something equally nasty. No mouse traps so far, which is nice.

We get up, adding this morning's dirty dishes to last night's pile.

Housework keeps

"I'm going to have a shower love," I say. "Could you call up work and say I can't get off the toilet or something equally vile. The fewer questions they want to ask, the better."

She rolls her eyes. "Do I really have to call your creepy boss? Why don't you call them yourself and say I am really sick and need to be looked after? That will get you a few more days if you play your cards right."

I laugh, and tell her that's not a bad plan. I also remind her that she an evil mastermind, and that she should consider drawing up plans for a doomsday device.

The First Day

The water is warm and soothing on my skin.

I am standing contentedly in our shower, looking about at the numerous soaps and shampoos nearby with what can only be called confused amusement. Bach's Sonata No.1 in G Minor is playing loudly from a portable MP3 player, which is sitting on a glass shelf across the lapis blue tiled bathroom. I gingerly grasp a cake of Musgo Real, a Portuguese luxury soap and take a hesitant sniff. It smells of patchouli and vetiver. Very masculine, so I am guessing it is not of Audrey's personal stash.

My wash progresses slowly, its delay a combination of the addictive quality of a shower's relaxing ritual and the slow reintroduction to washing under hot, flowing water.

After a rather long time without what most readers would call a banal and familiar chore, it amazes me that you would simply stand there and get it over with. The steam is invigorating as I breathe it in. The various soapy fragrances are uplifting and ethereal. Water massages your back in a thousand tiny, gentle streams. You would lay down a lot of credits where I came from to get that kind of contentment.

After hearing a knock on the door followed by an amused enquiry as to whether I had fallen down the drain, I am reminded that I may have been at this a while. I turn off the water and dry myself with a thick, fluffy cotton towel. I then slip back into my dressing gown and regard my reflection in the mirror.

A young man's face stares back at me. Small blue eyes accented with sharp cheekbones and strong eyebrows. A rounded jaw with full lips and near white teeth. Brown hair darkened with dampness. Not bad really, better than a few days back anyway.

Feelings of elation and terror fight for my attention, a howling maelstrom inside my head. I clearly haven't even come close to getting a grip on my current situation. One moment I am full of joy at a life renewed, the next I am almost shaking with the oppressive inertia that accompanies such a tremendous change of circumstance. I come to the conclusion that the only way to get used to this is to dive right in, and try not to think too much about the preposterous insanity that surrounds my every step.

I relearn a new everyday routine by brushing my teeth. The almost overbearing combination of artificial sweetness and strong mint is not a pleasurable experience at all, nor can I say the brushing is exceptionally fun either. Still, there are no Pod-O-Cleans around here yet, and furthermore they might not ever exist in this new timeline (or whatever you would call it). The near-vicious scent of Bay Rhum attacks my nostrils as I generously splash on some aftershave, applied even though I omitted shaving beforehand. I will leave that tenuous voyage of scraped skin and blood for tomorrow.

I exit the bathroom with a feeling of some accomplishment. This early 21st living is in no way a chore, like so many from my past would state primly. I will concede that there is more work in doing basic things in this era, but at a greater reward. The taste of my morning coffee will attest to that. Bloody thing took ten minutes to make, slow for even this current time-line, but the results were unmatchable.

Time to face the day, and this time I am looking forward to it.

I look about the house for Audrey, and find her sitting at the computer checking her email. I cannot suppress a slight derisive snort at how ridiculous the machine looks. Cords are messily gathered into a bulky tower, which is making an annoying whirring noise from the cooling fans attempting to prevent the machine from melting . . . or something. It is a hard fact to grasp that machines like this eventually evolved into the shapers of a new humanity, indeed a new world.

I sit exultantly on a plush leather couch behind her, secretly gladdened that Audrey did not ask what I was scoffing at. It would be a hard thing to explain I think. It dawns on me that I will never be able to tell her about my reawakening, lest she commit me into a mental hospice with the best of intentions. This thought saddens me in an unexpectedly potent way. I had always shared everything with her, and a lifetime of attempting to suppress monumental secret is not a pleasing prospect by any means.

"So what do you want to do now, secretly-healthy Alan?" says Audrey, her eyes glued to the computer screen.

"Ummm . . ." I consider. "What is it like outside?"

She laughs. "Go check for yourself. You know how much of a softie I am with the cold."

"Fair enough."

I head to the back door, floorboards creaking under my bare feet. A cool, fresh breeze greets me as I step outside. The sun is out, letting off a tepid warmth that struggles to allay the coldness that surrounds me.

I walk onto the back lawn, its soft blades of grass covered in a layer of fine morning dew. The smell of sweet fruit gently floats towards me, and I close my eyes to locate its origins. A dense, scraggly bush squats defiantly along the back fence, showing off a heavy yield of ripe, plump berries.

I make my way over, deftly plucking a single blackberry. Impulsively, I squeeze the soft flesh until it bursts, raining dark, sweet juice over my hand. Such a luxury, such a privilege to be standing on this soft grass with a hand sodden in fruit pulp.

I am unused to such abundant nature within such easy reach.

I close my eyes and simply stand, letting my senses explore my surroundings with a hesitant glee. My body sways slightly as I experience a certain solidarity and serene contentment from the prospect of existing amidst such complicated beauty. I discover again the pleasure of nature's cacophony, the clash of elements that somehow form a steady balance. The wind carries the smells of eucalyptus from the nearby gum trees, as well as the lovingly acrid smoke of a well burning fireplace. The invisible rising tendrils of the crushed berry's scent cut through the gentle surrounding air, adding a sweet overtone to the morning chill. My thoughts ascend from physicality.

I recall a revelation I had not too long ago, perhaps from the wisdom that comes slowly over a lifetime, or merely because of the conditions in which I existed. I discovered that your life is not on exhibition for others to judge. We do so many things just to please other people, or worse, to portray to others what kind of person we are. You find yourself being pigeon-holed into a specific identity, and being forced to dress and act the part. How many times do you hear people saying "I just want to be myself!"? Yet do they have the courage to do so?

I will, this time.

The time for pretence is far behind me, lost when my identity became obscured amidst the misery of forced retirement. There was no parade, no competition in our old age, because we had all stopped playing that awful game. I see no reason I cannot bring that freedom of self back into this new life. There will be no acquiescence to the absurd social system, no meek submission to the twisted politics of companionship. As I stand outside, connected to this world in an almost symbiotic way, I vow to simply enjoy it all. Screw the judgment of those who could never judge themselves, it will not concern me at all this second time around.

Work will be interesting, I chuckle to myself.

This is the first day in a new life, and I am not taking for granted one single moment of this astounding opportunity. The events of yesterday have opened my eyes to the fleeting chance at happiness we are given before the world is rid of us forever. Usually we get but one try at life in the short time we are granted, and I am lucky enough to have two.

What person could live their lives bound by horrible restrictions a second time around? What person would sacrifice so much for others simply to be viewed upon with fleeting favor? To live a life as if on show for all to see?

Certainly not me. I muse as I make my way over to the garden tap.

The splash of cold water on my hands temporarily revives me from my musings and I begrudgingly start to scrub the hardening maroon berry stains from my skin. I hear my internal monologue fight once more for full attention.

I consider, as my hands drip clear water to the pavement below, that while I will not do anything to harm Audrey's chance at happiness, neither will I do anything to lessen my own chance to live well. It is my responsibility to myself to heighten the pleasure and lessen the pain of life, as it is Audrey's responsibility to do so for her own. We can certainly walk the same path, but I cannot be her navigator, as she cannot be mine.

Maybe my old age has made me selfish, yet it has also helped me learn that that is not a flaw. Everyone is selfish. Good deeds come from the joy that is derived from helping others, rather than some natural instinct. A person that sacrifices their last drop of water for someone else in a desert storm is either a martyr or madly blinded by love.

Of course, one can be too self centered to the detriment of others, but I think that is merely a person out of balance with their own nature. We are a communal species, and sacrificing the good of all for the benefit of one is not natural. After all, you may have all the food in the village, but who is going to help you fend off the wolves if your tribe has starved to death?

I take my time walking back inside, and spy Audrey sketching by the lounge room window. Her lips are parted in concentration, and she does not notice me standing by the door to the room.

"It's not too bad out there love," I say softly. "Do you want to draw outside in the sun?"

She looks up distractedly. "Ummm, alright . . . as long as it's not too chilly. Let me get my jacket."

We spend the day together, relaxed and relishing our time together. We make love, we watch a pirated movie on the computer, we eat a decadent homemade pizza, we listen to loud music in our study while Audrey finishes her sketch. I could not have wished for a gentler, more pleasurable day to start my new life with. Time passes quickly, happiness washing over me in a viridian haze.

I never remembered life being this perfect, this serene. The thousand tiny details of each day bloom with the resurgence of renewed observance. I often unwittingly pause to slowly take it all in, and then catch myself before I linger too long.

If Audrey has noticed these odd retractions and random reflections, she hasn't mentioned it yet. I wonder more than once if she will. The shock of being an old man in a young man's body is hard enough to discover for oneself, but to realize that the one you hold dearest to your heart is suddenly a different person would be a challenge in extremity.

I hope that she never notices the change.

Applications

The air feels heavy and still.

I am sitting awkwardly on an uncomfortable plastic chair, looking at everything but my boss as he is attempting light banter. We are in the cramped staff kitchen, sitting at a shamefully stained table across from one other. Greasy, crumpled fast food wrapping is strewn haphazardly about his resting arms. I notice how out of place my cold homemade pizza, neatly wrapped in aluminum foil, must look to him.

"So how are you feeling?" he asks in a condescending tone. "All better now?"

"I wasn't sick; it was Audrey who needed looking after." I reply noncommittally, finding myself feeling rather unconcerned in garnering his approval.

"Of course." I note the heavy use of sarcasm. "I take it she is fine now?"

"Well enough for me to be back here." I can't believe it is Monday already.

"Yes, good." The intermittent flicker of the overly effulgent fluorescent lighting begins to grind away at my patience at its every pulse. I cannot even begin to grasp at how I had the willpower to put up with this loud and disgusting person ordering me around five days a week.

I glance around the room for what seems like the hundredth time, taking in the tacky decor with bemusement. Huge orange triangle shapes are stuck garishly on the white wall near the refrigerator in a cheap effort to brighten the drab room. I guess this passed for modern and trendy in my past, but perhaps not even then. Employee notices and procedures coat the walls in a display of banality and oblique workplace jargon.

"Pizza good?" the boss asks with a greasy smile. "I'm surprised you had the time to make such a lavish meal when you had to look after your wife yesterday."

"It's not hard to do, and she was sleeping at the time," I state dismissively.

"Right, no . . . Sure," comes the quiet reply. "We need to talk later on about your team's sales quota for this month, could you come by my office this afternoon?"

"Yeah, no problems Craig," I placate apathetically.

"Good." He slides off the seat and saunters off; leaving his discarded takeout wrapper speckled with lettuce and tomato chunks in front of me. For the entire morning at work I have been walking around in somewhat of a daze, the oppressive atmosphere of stress and brittle laughter is a renewed experience I could have done without. Everyone here is either on an over caffeinated rollercoaster of smiles and vacant stares, or they are detached from how their day progresses in an almost surreal way.

I suppose it never impacted me in such a manner before because I was used to it all, the anesthetic of repetition softens even the hardest of circumstances. Now I find myself with that veil of staid numbness torn asunder, my reawakening providing me with a fresh perspective. It is as though a bright and searing light is being shone down a dark alleyway for the first time in years. Rats scurry away in its glare as pockets of filth are lit in stark and honest detail. There is no longer a blanket of muted shadows in which to soften the overbearing putrescence, merely the unyielding honesty of crisp illumination.

I listen to the feigned energetic voices of those seated around me. Some discuss how outraged they were to receive the wrong model hair straightener from eBay, while others exchange slurred discourse on the most effective way to sneak booze into a cinema. I see the quiet types sitting alone, heads crammed between the pages of cheap fantasy novels. They are desperately trying not to notice the clock on the wall slowly ticking its way towards their return to reality. I smell the stale, almost sickening aromas of old food, coffee and tea stains that the apathetic cleaner's tattered rag has not removed. Most of all I feel. I feel the heavy fog of oppressive sadness cling to anyone who enters it, suffocating life with each pore it smothers.

Misery gilded with pretension is all I see surrounding me. People gliding around vacuously, cramming the empty void within their broken minds with shallow distractions and expensive weekends soaked in amnesiaic alcohol. I wonder if it could be any other way for them, or for me. Did I live like this, and simply not realize?

Aristotle once stated that we are what we repeatedly do. What did that make me? What does that make all these empty vessels that surround me? The answer keeps surfacing in my mind no matter how many times I try and drown it away:

Nothing.

I begin to doubt if I will be able to come to this miserable haven of stress and affectation for the majority of every week, yet at the same time I realize that in this era income has a high priority. Simple human needs such as shelter and food cannot be met unless you give your life away in meek subservience. To cage myself in willingly to this bizarre circus act seems preposterous to me now that I have been away from it for so long. It dawns on me that perhaps there is a different path for me to explore in this new life. The fear of change that paralyzed me in my structured and predictable past seems laughable now, considering how much has changed in the last couple of days.

I know one person in my life that will be able to help me find my way on this new path, and she is sitting at home right now. Audrey is a freelance illustrator, taking jobs for children's books and advertising firms alike. The irregular hours and possible months without steady work never bothered her as it did me. I took this job as a security blanket, but I realize now that it was entirely for my own satiation. Audrey would not have cared if I was working one day a year as a balloon artist for the Prime Minister. All she ever wanted was for me to be happy, and not stress so much.

I get the feeling she will be getting her wish much more this time around.

The allotted time for my lunch ends, and I head back to my office to attempt to hide from the cacophony of the call centre as best I can. The door clicks closed quietly, and I notice with relief that the constant noise of hands thumping on keyboards and the accompanying mono-toned sales pitch gets muted perceptively. Taking a deep breath, I move over to my desk and once again find myself seated. It seems there is a lot of sitting involved in office work.

Adrenaline surges unbidden as I count the minutes before someone will notice my absence from around the snapshot-ridden cubicles of my overworked sales team. I was usually a constant fixture, urging them to reach higher targets and answering the same questions over and over again. I wonder if they will simply enjoy the luxury of my not standing over their shoulders.

I distract myself with exploring the joyously primitive Internet. It is raw, uncensored and full of potential. It had turned into a restrained and lifeless propaganda machine in my time, and had lost all that had made it wonderful: the free exchange of ideas and information.

At my fingertips is the last bastion of free speech in the world. I remember that when it got privatized, it was no longer possible to access any unbiased information from that point onwards. I find myself more than slightly amazed at the sheer excess and availability of any data requested. Sure, it is a crude collection of web pages barely strung together with the help of clumsy search engines, but it is amazing in its absolute size and prowess. Before I can even type in something childish into Google, my office phone rings shrilly, cutting through the tranquility of my snatched solace.

"Alan, Craig here."

"Hi," I reply in a monotone.

"Look, could you come up so we could discuss some things?"

"Now?"

"Yes, Alan, if you wouldn't mind coming now that would be super," he says in a clipped tone. I use my faded memory to guide me hesitantly to his office door three floors up. I cannot recall how many times I had made that trip, but I always made a point to put it out my mind as soon as it was over. I believe this will be no exception.

Craig is the epitome of this era's faux-friendly boss. Greased smiles and subtly dirty stories abound, with tactless critiques sandwiched between awkward compliments whenever he assesses your worth. I have little doubt that this will be another poorly executed pep-talk to try and get me to do the same to those working under me. The chain reaction of pressure from one level of management to the next is predictably humorous as much as it is annoying.

Throughout the progression of this day, I have gone from a shocked observance to a brooding sadness. The curse of spending your day in an environment not of your choosing is that you do anything to make the day speed by, merely so you can head home for a few hours reprieve. This in turn makes you forget all the mindless drudgery you have accomplished, notwithstanding the memorably bad parts. The end result of this is that by retirement, you have forgotten just how bad everything was on an hour-to-hour basis. Imagine being reinserted into such a situation after putting all that pleasantly behind you.

It is wholly disheartening, if you hadn't guessed as much.

I arrive at his door in dejected silence. There is little motivating me to raise my hand and knock. I consider turning around and walking away, out the door and straight home grinning ear to ear, but before I can, I hear Craig call out at me to come in. Well, a frosted glass panel on the door would give me away slightly, wouldn't it?

I walk into his domain; his room almost identical to mine, save it is slightly bigger and has different personal effects on cluttered on his desk and walls. Come to think of it, most of the rooms in this building are the same. Light grey walls, cheap furnishings and annoying fluorescent lights. Everything here announces its cheap utilitarianism in a monumental way. I sit unceremoniously without being prompted.

Craig regards me with narrowed eyes, seething thoughts running rampant behind his gaze. He certainly likes being in charge, and even this little breach of protocol has gotten him riled up. I suppress a chuckle at his expense.

"Alan, glad you could make it."

"Craig."

"I'm going to speak plainly if I may."

"Sure."

"I have been going over last month's sales," he begins in his best relaxed, professional tone. "While your team has made target, I cannot help but feel you guys can be getting more contracts renewed in the future."

My poor sales team. Their job is customer retention. It is a hard enough ask to try and convince a customer to stay with our company when they have called up to leave for greener pastures, but by the time they get to speaking with one of my team they have already been transferred twice. That makes my team the third point of contact amidst the endless sea of call-waiting, forcing a long delay in the completion of what should be a simple task. Stress is high on both ends of the phone by the end of the conversation, and it is rare when we get someone to stay on. I am amazed we are reaching the target quota at all.

"What would you have me try?" I query, breaking protocol by staring straight at him as I talk.

"I recently won this little TV set at a quiz night," he says, pointing to a small box perched on top of a filing cabinet. "I thought I could donate it to you guys if you make thirty percent above your quota. Sounds good right?"

"That's a thirty-four centimeter TV Craig," I respond wearily as I look upon the small cardboard box. "Does anyone even use analogue sets these days?"

"Well, not a great deal of people, no. Maybe you could go and buy a digital set-top box to go with it?" He attempts a casual smile, yet only succeeds in looking as though he has spontaneously herniated. "That should peak some interest."

"I don't really think that is going to motivate even the simplest of my staff Craig, not that relic. What kind of quiz night was this?" I suppress a sigh.

"Alan, I don't think your attitude is a productive one at present." My boss is visibly struggling to maintain his sassy-cool facade. "I am offering real incentive for your team to improve quota and you are flatly refusing."

"How about an iPod?"

"I have a telly."

"Well, I don't think a set top box will sweeten this deal anyway. I don't think I will be bothering with that."

"Bothering with that?" Craig retorts acid-tongued. "Perhaps I shouldn't be bothered with your bonus this year? Perhaps I shouldn't be bothered with employing you at all?"

"Because I won't purchase a set top box to go with your antique?"

"Be reasonable Alan, it's a free prize."

"Not for me it isn't," I interrupt. I notice my trademark politeness has dissipated in the wake of this obnoxious assault.

He pauses, regarding me with a curious expression. "Alan, I feel that your lack of helpfulness in this matter is indicative of your lack of motivation overall with this job."

That's a far leap. I think to myself.

Was it always the case that you do absolutely everything your boss tells you to do; otherwise you get threatened with the sack? What a power they would wield if that was indeed a factual assumption. "Don't you think that is jumping a bit far ahead?" I say, merely for the sake of interest.

"No Alan, no I do not," Craig states simply, seemingly enjoying the perceived panic my protest implies. He laps up misery like a starved wolf, licking his swollen lips in anticipation of my backing down. "Why on earth wouldn't you be interested in motivating your team further?"

"If I were interested in motivating them, I believe that attempting to buy them out with my grandmother's kitchen TV would insult them more than anything else," I state flatly, thoroughly enjoying bucking the model-employee trend. "Furthermore, insisting that because I don't want to pawn your junk means I hate my job is strange to say the least."

This game is beginning to get fun. Before now I had never felt brave enough to talk to my boss like a normal person, treating him instead like some sort of infallible commander. The prospect of staying here under such a subservient sway is does not run parallel with my new lease on life. Either he decides to treat me with even a small amount of decency or I walk away from this ridiculous place with contented ease.

"Listen, Alan," he jumps in suddenly. "You are making this far too complicated. Either you play ball, or you can go home without half-time oranges."

"Half-time oranges?" I cannot help displaying open confusion at this. This is clearly a man who is so used to the flittering, fragile smiles of an entourage of sycophants that he actually believes himself to witty.

"Do you want this job or not? I know plenty of people who would consider it lucky having such responsibility and high salary," Craig lectures haughtily. "Now either shape up or ship out."

I consider the uncanny proposal that is being made to me. I either bow down and submit to even the most bizarre whims of my boss, or I get fired. This includes bribing my staff with a shitty television set, and paying out of my own pocket to make it actually usable in a modern context. I have a sneaking suspicion that Craig could easily weasel out of any unfair dismissal accusation I could bring to bear, but to actually care about that would suggest that I am in some way attached to my current job. That may have been the case for poor old Alan, before this older and wiser version invaded his mind, but things are different now.

It's all about me now. My happiness.

"Got a ticket for that cruise then Craig?" Bad puns are always the most fun.

"What cruise?" he asks incredulously, his eyes full of suspicion. "Have you gone off the deep end?"

"You said for me to ship out. I'll take that offer if you don't mind terribly," I state calmly, a feeling of warmth imbuing me for the first time since yesterday. It is as though the clammy, cold suffocation that has plagued me since my arrival today has been washed away in a flood of free will made manifest. "I might leave straight away actually, don't worry about the holiday pay, I just used all that up last month if I remember correctly."

His manner changes instantly, from threatening to placating. "Now don't be rash Alan," he begins, but I am already standing. There are better ways to spend one's life than to be the lackey of an utter fool and pretend to enjoy it.

I tell him as much as I walk out the door.

Uncertainty

As I step outside, the world seems brighter and more fresh.

It has been mere minutes since I quietly slipped away from that derogating dungeon that I had called a job. Standing with the sliding glass entrance to the tall soulless skyscraper behind me, I look around as if I am seeing these familiar surrounds in a new light. Dizzying elation and hot pangs of doubt surge through my every limb, filling me with adrenaline that refuses to meekly subside.

In the back of my mind I know that the heady, intoxicating fuel of pure freedom can only engorge me for but a fleeting duration before I crash into a sobering pit of doubt and bitter hindsight. This thought flickers in the recesses of my consciousness like a stubborn candle in a strong wind, barely bright enough to garner my full attention whilst I am so distracted with joy. Already I can hear my sensible side loading logical reprimands into its conscience-cannons to do battle with the wild and untamed part of me who simply craves hedonistic chaos.

I begin my blissful meandering through town, heart pumping furiously in response to this long latent and brash desire made corporeal. I am near Rundle Street, the beginning of the vertical streak of adjoined streets that make up the hub of the city of Adelaide. They are full of small, quirky cafes and independent stores, each offering a varied and unique experience that is not found with such abundance in larger cities. I plan to distract and envelop my senses in the sights and sounds of a small and vibrant city before heading home and attempting to chart a new course in these murky waters of change.

I notice a relaxed-looking wine bar as I slowly wander down the street; small groups of quiet socialites gathered at the tables outside, enjoying the mild weather and each other's presence. I consider stopping here, finding a spot in the tepid sunlight in order to watch the traffic

slowly pass me by, like a rock amidst the lapping waters
of an incoming tide. Yet it feels too early to for such a
reprieve. I have just started my exalted exploration, and
the need for such a calm oasis has not yet arrived. I walk
by, absorbing all the tiny details, and vowing to come
back to this very place as soon as I feel the urge.

Crossing the road, I stroll pass some busy cafes that
seem to scream out for attention, the polar opposite of
the wine bar I had just encountered. Garlic and sweet
onion aromas roll around outside under the verandah,
blending with the bouncing tones of contented and lo-
quacious diners. Huge serves of pasta are heaped on bold
white plates, with even the most ravenous of eaters not
feeling up to the challenge of finishing the hefty meals.
I squeeze through the awkwardly gathered pedestrians
who have stopped to talk to acquaintances they have
spotted eating alfresco, often to the diner's chagrin, and
make my way onwards.

What strikes me more than most aspects of this bus-
tling sidewalk is the bright and bold usage of colors on
display at every opportunity. I see an old stone building painted matte black with a bright red sign above
the entrance in a perfect splash of color, each extreme
emphasizing the other. It is striking in its simplicity and
rather classy to look at. Other shops are painted bright
yellow, or turquoise, with the odd cream and grey facade to break up the kaleidoscope of color.

Public art is imaginative as well as traditional. A mu-
ral covers an entire side of a building, paint faded and
chipped with the passage of time.

More contemporary art is literally stuck into the sidewalk in the form of thousands of coins, teasing the passerby with their immovability. Compared to where I was
but a few days before, this is a veritable riot of color and
imagination let loose.

It amazes me to see the mass of oblivious patrons
and brisk businessmen with their faces fused to fancy

phones, apathetically numb to their surrounds. I am once again reminded of how much of a stranger I am in my own past, the product of the sterile and banal future from which I came. A thought spurs to mind that it may be some time before I will adjust and adapt, letting my memories and my present become symbiotic, or if indeed they will merge at all.

The rich, earthy odor of tobacco softly tugs at my nostrils as I pass a genuine tobacconist. I stop in surprise at the appearance of an actual smoke shop, and not one of those conglomerated gift stores with more Teddy bears than cigarettes to be found on the shelves. A mental cog turns and whirs into place as my memory buffers the reality before me. I used to come here once a week when I was younger than even this version of me was, and purchase three or four cigars to go in my humidor. This was before I discovered the pleasure that is pipe smoking.

I remember before the indoor smoking ban, the owner used to sit behind the back counter and contentedly puff on his own pipe, letting his son take care of sales while he took a well-earned break. I also recall his sheer disgust at the ban when it was implemented, grumbling that people who willingly enter a tobacconist should know full well what to expect when they walk through the door, that that banning smoking there was just going too far.

A strong desire compels me to enter this haven of old world vice, and experience again the primal pleasure of fire and burning leaf. I know that I have a small collection of smoking pipes are gathered in my den at home, but I have not yet dared to begin this ritual anew. I linger at the doorway, weighing up my desire to enter versus the trepidation of encountering another familiar face with the distance of time obfuscating social ease.

I grit my teeth and go inside, feeling the pangs of awkwardness follow me past the threshold.

"Alan," says a voice before I am halfway past the first counter. "Don't usually see you until Wednesday. To what do I owe the pleasure of your company?"

It is Geoffrey, the owner and proprietor of my old haunt. I look around at the small yet cozy store. To my right are display cabinets showing off quality humidor and smoking accessories as well as a few vending machines to cater for the late night shopper. Across from that, to my left is a hoard of tobacco products. Displayed on the back wall are various brands of cigarettes, machine made cigarillos, pouches of loose leaf and tins of pipe tobacco neatly arranged. An entire shelf near back is devoted to large jars with white stickers that contain house-blended pipe tobacco of which I used to always enjoy sampling. Taking pride of place in front of that wall, and also doubling as the front-counter of the store, is a humidified cabinet displaying a large selection of Cuban and imported cigars. Wood trim and polished glass are prominent, making the store feel welcoming and relaxed.

"Just passing by, thought I would come in and have a look."

"Sure, no complaints here." He smiles slowly, and moves to serve someone asking for a pack of Benson and Hedges. I remember always having to pause our conversations for the steady trickle of cigarette lovers zipping in and out for their fix. Such a distraction is more aptly labeled a reprieve at present, as I have no idea what to say to this acquaintance from a bygone era. Snatching the opportunity the impatient customer has provided me, I wander to the back of the store and simply absorb the ambience of such a long forgotten place.

This type of store, as well as liquor stores, porn shops, casinos and other so-called havens of sin and debauchery were simply not seen in my future. The slow progression of minor policy change and then the bans that followed them rolled steadily on until there was practically nothing left to outlaw. It was all done in tiny increments, saturated with governmental campaigns professing concern for the proverbial children, and enabling the social ostracism of those who chose not to be pushed away from pursuing legal hobbies.

Junk science and blatant lies were the currency of said propaganda, with too few actually bothering to stop and question what they saw on the television. By the time we all took a collective look around us and saw we had nothing left, it was far too late. I remember being annoyed even in this decade at our freedoms been slowly chipped away, the product of an overly paranoid string of governments bent on utter control. But what did I know of it? I couldn't do a thing about it then, and I will not try to do anything about it now. I will simply enjoy whatever freedoms this era offers and hope the song doesn't play the same way this second time around.

"Sorry about that Alan," Geoffrey says with a warm smile. "What can I do for you today?"

I inwardly cringe, not really remembering well enough how this ritual went. "Are there any blends I have yet to sample?" I bluff, secretly very pleased at my quick thinking.

I see him consider briefly, hand tapping slowly on his chin. "You could try Flamenco," he offers. "A very rich aromatic blend. Smells like dark chocolate. Here, have a whiff."

He moves over to a jar fairly high up and brings it down, needing two hands to support its weight. A soft clink announces the open lid, and I lower my nose to smell the loose tobacco. It is heady, earthy and does indeed remind me of very dark chocolate. Not sweet, but creamy and complex with traces of licorice and pea straw. Such delight. I know it may taste entirely different to how it smells, but I have the feeling I will not be let down. Once again I find myself thanking James for convincing me to embark on this wild journey.

"Smells good," I say hurriedly. "Could I get some?"

Geoffrey grins. "No, I was showing you so you could go home saddened and without anything to fill your pipe with."

I laugh as he fills a small plastic pouch with a carefully weighted amount of Flamenco that was measured on a large set of scales. He doesn't even mention the price out loud, just motions to the display on the cashier that indicates I must part with $14.25. I comply, marveling at the tiny amount of money I need to hand over for such an indulgence. We part ways, smiling politely. Slowly I weave past the queue of calamitous cravers of dangerous vices and pass into the brightness of daylight.

I am very nearly knocked over as I exit the tobacconist by a towering, muscle-bound man dressed rather inappropriately for a mid-Autumn day.

"Sorry mate," he apologizes in a warm tone as I stare at his garish singlet advertising some sort of foreign beer, then down to his brightly patterned shorts. "You alright bro?"

"Err . . ." I manage to reply quietly, my heart beating at the unexpected physical intrusion. Standing so close to this imposing man, I briefly get the impression that his shoulders block out the sunlight itself. "Yeah, no problems."

"Here mate, you hungry?" the stranger says as he hands me what I imagine is the greasiest taco I have ever held. A chunk of barely warm meat works its way out of the soggy shell and splatters onto my shoe. "No hard feelings."

"Wait . . ." I begin, but he has already stridently moved away down the sidewalk, leaving me clutching his abandoned lunch. I take a few moments to compose myself, then make my way over to a bin.

Such a random encounter would have been simply unthinkable in my old life, but despite the unutterable strangeness of what has just occurred, I can't help a deep, amused chuckle from escaping my lips.

What an era to come back to!

Firmly grasping the plastic pouch of tobacco in my hand as I resume my sojourn, the potential pleasures that this divergent course can offer me anew suddenly seem more tangible. What other simple delights will my newly attentive soul experience during the course of everyday life? How long before I become numbed by their pleasure, adapting and becoming flippant with their ease of obtainability? Will I let myself become so complacent, knowing the future that may be lying in wait for me?

I inhale deeply through my nose, taking in the myriad of smells that surround a busy street and vow to cling on to the beauty of this complexity for as long as my mind will let me.

The weight of the little parcel in my hands seems to increase every time I let my mind drift back to my snap decision to leave a stable job behind in the pursuit of happiness. What if my newly rediscovered love for a hedonistic imperative does not walk easily down the same path of vocational contentment? Is having a high paying job necessary for indulging in life's best offerings, or do people in top jobs turn to those vices to escape the huge pressures that comes with such undertakings? I am not at all certain of which is closer to the truth. Surely I must find a balance, but at the moment the hot surges of doubt from the pit of my stomach do naught but inform me of the absence of such equilibrium.

Once again I reach the conclusion that I am lost in this era of circumstantial self-navigation, that I will need the help of someone who is excellent at charting her own course. With a rather unusual efflux of willpower I manage to push those thoughts to the back of my mind, at least until I get home and can cling to the support of my calm and efficacious Audrey.

As I reach Rundle Mall; a busy strip of brightly lit conglomerate stores and the accompanying plethora of poxy advertisements, I am taken aback at how the charm of the city seems drowned out amidst such glaring capitalism. Beautiful stone facades are treated with contempt by glossy glass storefronts, blocking their timeworn glory with garish neon fixtures.

People seem more rushed here, striding past each doorway with a purposeful sneer. An intrusive voice is carried through crackling speakers, practically demanding each passerby enter the store he is hawking and be amazed at the twenty percent savings. I hear him address individuals that are unfortunate enough to enter his field of vision and attempt to embarrass them into entering. "Aren't you going to buy your beautiful wife some new cutlery sir?" he demands vociferously. I shake my head in disbelief and cross to the other side of the mall.

I notice how some people seem to be competing in how important they look, affecting an unerring pride in their grey suits and matching haircuts. Others seem strident in their supposed individuality, making a point to be seen as strange and different. It is an unusual mix of clashing ideals, and looks to my jaded old mind like some sort of twisted parade. I look closer, and notice the people who have no desire to stand out are harder to spot, they simply melt away under the heat of the supercharged egos that surround them.

The noise, the glares of self important businessmen, the jostling of teenagers attempting not to look like they want the entire world's attention for themselves. The promotional music blasting out of retail stores and hairdressing salons alike, the busker getting annoyed that nobody has stopped to pay him for his time in half an hour. It is all becoming too much stimulation to take in at once. The small cafe with a long line of peroxide-blond poseurs, snarling and backstabbing whomever is unlucky enough to be absent. The older man yelling at a clerk for bringing down the wrong shoe box, his spittle spraying the poor girls face. A married couple arguing vehemently over whose turn it is to drive the Mercedes to their friend's dinner party . . .

Yet as I peer past the forced expressions collectively displayed on strained faces, I see that there is an underlying sadness here. A misery that reverberates throughout the jubilant signage and glossy print that saturates every wall. Generously applied makeup can do little to hide the bags under weary eyes, nor does an expensive suit conceal a defeated slump. This ominous pretense hides just out of plain sight, manifesting in dollar figures on cardboard signs like the modern equivalent of a carrot on a string. It manages to pull a deluge of vagrant spenders to its cold and calculating embrace, uncaring at the fact that they walk away as unhappy as they arrived (but usually with less money).

I cannot help but notice the hundreds of vacant stares that glide over the brightened facades, examining a stream of information in a heartbeat, yet absorbing none of the tangible reality before them. Here is a well lit and carefully planned dungeon that does not need physical bars across the windows to keep its denizens imprisoned, but merely the bars on a dollar sign.

Humanity is, at this moment, disgusting and saddening. A horrid display of empty vessels throwing cash around like dizzy monkeys with a handful of semen, shaking their heads at each other in a uniform display of disapproval. I do not know if it is the mall attracting the shallowest of people, or if they simply stand out much more in a collective environment.

This writhing throng of consumers is an experience I was not prepared for. I narrowly avoid getting ice-cream deposited apathetically on my suit by an inattentive shopper, then almost run into a group of angry looking teens, faces caked in makeup and contorted with contrived sneers.

I have had enough of this for now. It is far too much to go from a quiet, mind numbing existence to being dumped amidst this pulsating chaos. This is clearly something I will have to get used to once more. Perhaps this is one thing I will willingly let myself adapt to, to numb its overwhelming nature with the placation of familiarity. I'd imagine the first time a child gets lost in a busy room would feel very similar to what I do now.

I make my way quickly to the bus stop and find a spot to sit on a low wall behind the crowded shelter. I am not looking forward to being stuffed into an antiquated rust-bucket on wheels for forty five minutes, breathing in the stagnant air of a hundred mouths. What does soothe me however, is the prospect of being away from all that damned noise that seemed to follow me from that overcrowded mass of vacuous humanity.

I notice with grim humor that my wild and untamed side that craves hedonistic chaos is strangely silent.

It is going to be a long ride home.

A Dream

Thick cotton rot crumbles slowly.

Oozing tar seeps gingerly through gentle gaps in the brittle walls. Hesitant darkened rivers weave tiny paths as they approach the floor's embrace. Writhing and twisting. Serpentine.

Clouds of thick red confusion wend inwardly through strained and watery eyes, choking elementary perceptions. An unceasing drone of mechanical discontent reverberates throughout my core, apathetically reaching for undivided attention.

Watery yellow droplets rain uniformly sideways past immobile arms. In a searing flash of orange, they morph into hot, dancing sparks that whirl in a chaotic spiral floating ever upwards to the sagging roof. Pulses of unyielding brightness cut through the muted fog, blinding my searching gaze with sharp agony.

Warmth envelops me in a sticky red heat that grows chill as it soaks my torn clothing. Soft, restraining hands wrap purposely around my weakened body, embracing me in a determined lust. I struggle to gain purchase, heaving in panic against the old and leathery skin that ensnares me. A groan escapes my captor's breath as I struggle, yet the pressure on my chest does not lessen.

My eyes stay closed longer each time they black out their surrounds. Weak lids heave against the invisible threads of fatigue that bind them tightly shut.

Thick, acrid smoke rolls around the room, lost and meandering. It lazily claws its thin tendrils up my nose, forcing my heavy head to turn away and meekly cough in protest.

Ragged perception loses its grip as my heart beats slower and more loudly in my ears.

I drift.

Textured plastic grips fleetingly at my sensitive outstretched skin. I recoil weakly with blurred vision, but my eyes cannot make contact with the weathered phantom that looms over me.

Muted dull roars thump irregularly around my motionless body while white static hisses at me from above in electronic discontent. Objects fade from view, shrinking as if from fear before my fatigued comprehension.

Midnight-black looms ominously, waiting to descend upon the fading realm of which I inhabit. I hear panicked voices scraping down the flaking walls, skittering like energetic insects from one spot to another.

The corporeal lessens its hold on me as I melt slowly into the stiff, concrete grip that restrains my every physical protest.

Silky violet ribbons dance before me, then slither into the awaiting darkness, beckoning my mind to follow. They writhe in a liquid display, flirting with the inky blackness that is steadily engulfing all in its path.

Blurred lines and incomplete forms reward my confused glare as I attempt for the last time to gain solidarity. Above me, the sensuous, crisp display grows brighter, and I make my choice.

I follow them away from this painful place, their gravity caressing and pulling me at a jolting pace towards the dark unknown. Elation surges in place of receding panic and I let myself be led towards their destination.

Reflections

The night is calm and lonely.

I am sitting in front of a computer monitor, staring blankly at the blinking cursor that awaits my input with infinite patience. Of course, now that I have typed that sentence I can see my thoughts in their pixelized form; the transient thoughts inside my head transformed into distilled permanence.

After awakening from a vivid and somewhat terrifying dream, I found I could not return to sleep easily. Perhaps I was simply too frightened to attempt such casual flippancy? The soft whirr of my computer's primitive cooling fans and the steady tick of a wall clock perched behind me are the only things keeping me company on this otherwise silent vigil.

The yellowed artificial brightness of invasive twenty-first century lighting beams down, illuminating with pulsating intensity the desk at which I am perched. Wrappers from hastily consumed chocolate bars are strewn carelessly next to an empty bottle of coke, adding to the clutter surrounding them with juxtaposed impunity.

After attempting to simply distract myself from my loud and demanding thoughts with meaningless Internet stumbling, the nagging urge to organize and examine this chaos surging from within my head became too strong to ignore. I have typed out the events of the past week, from the day I met James again to right now: an hour after that strange dream.

I do not know whether doing so was in fact a prudent decision, for if Audrey ever discovered my audacious rantings I would not know what to say or do. Perhaps I could simply act bashful and ask if she likes my novel? Hopefully I can stop her reaching this particular paragraph should that event occur.

So here we meet again, dear reader. I do not know who you are, or indeed why I am addressing you, but I feel that this story must be told to somebody . . . If only for the sole reason of someone else sharing with me what is more and more starting to feel like a modern Odyssey. If another person can experience what I am now, despite that it is by proxy alone, perhaps I can give purpose to this selfish journey of life lived anew? To validate this amazing opportunity by letting you see what I saw of this complex and fascinating period of time, through the eyes of someone who had thought such dizzying possibilities lost forever.

Whatever the reason of us meeting here on this page, and those to follow, I would be most pleased if this narrative inspires you to look at the world with renewed vigor. To realize that you live in a period of immense possibility, despite the ferocious nature of humanity and the misery that brings. If I could take one lesson from my own past (which may or may not be your future), it would be that when all of life's danger has been removed, so goes all of what makes it a pleasure to live. Perhaps it is the conquering of adversity that really makes us appreciate the bounties that result? When there is nothing left to fear, we stagnate and lose motivation. Or at least I did. The dreadful feeling of being little more than driftwood; powerless to the surging currents that clumsily steer your path, is not one I wish to be encompassed with again.

Thankfully, the tides of banality are only just stirring in this era, meekly lapping at the heels of the soft-minded. I will dizzily gorge upon the dying fruits of liberty before they shrivel and die away.

Enough self-righteous ranting.

I know how much I hated being lectured throughout my life, and I should probably refrain from telling you how to think and feel. Age does bring wisdom, but wisdom is wasted on the young.

All I really want is for you to appreciate how lucky you are to be alive at this magnificent time. Take from my journey what you will, and hopefully something in these pages sparks a fire within you.

***

The floorboards creak in noisy complaint as I attempt to walk quietly to the study. I have saved my story thus far in a folder hidden within Window's system files and happily put the whining computer out of its misery for the night. It feels good to have put these wild and sprawling thoughts down in a somewhat ordered fashion. My mind seems quieter now; more willing to embrace the reality before me now that I have managed to address the confounding events of my recent past.

I look down to the elegant blue and cream patterned rug on the study floor and laugh out loud at the criss-crossing, silvery trails of a solitary slug that is now motionless in the centre of his masterpiece. It is paralyzed with fear in the sudden brightness.

I gingerly step over it and brush away some of the fine silver slime with one of my brown-slippered feet. It comes off easily, and I chuckle again at this audacious gastropod. It strikes me that most people would sneer and complain about how their precious carpet is being sullied by this simple creature, but I am secretly pleased that this slimy little bastard has woven me a picture that Pollock would have be proud to call his own. I would have loved a bit of unexpected slug-induced levity in my previous life . . . anything to break up the monotony.

Leaving him to it, I step over to my dark wooden hutch.

I open the top left door and look at the contents with a child-like amazement. Casually staring back at me is a collection of amber spirits that would have gotten me in a sizeable cauldron of hot water if I were in possession of them back when my hair was grey. Glenrothes 1992 scotch, Tariquet VSOP Armagnac, Appleton Estate rum,

Maker's Mark bourbon. I am sure you get the picture without me naming them all. I recall many moments when I would have gone a week without the Pod-O-Clean to get two fingers of amber excellence. Here they all are before me, as if patiently waiting all these years for me to return and pour out a dram.

This pleasing illusion is shattered as I look down and see a crystal tumbler, clouded with fingerprints, sitting on the counter of the hutch. It seems as though my previous self has indulged not too long ago.

My turn.

I grasp the bottle of Glenrothes 1992 scotch with reverential awe and set it down next to my humidor. My conscience has been pestering me to try out that pipe tobacco blend I randomly purchased at the tobacconist yesterday, but as I open the lid of the walnut burl box, I quickly cast aside such thoughts.

A small, bright red tin catches my eye, instantly making me reach for it and hold it in the light. Depicted on the top of the label is an English red-robed judge in a horsehair wig smoking a pipe. Below him is a black oval that reads *Orlik* in white lettering, and under that *pipe tobacco* in small yellow writing.

Memories of my sitting silently on the nearby leather couch instantly surface, the specter of my past waiting patiently for me to rejoin him in solace. I recall my carved Meerschaum pipe stuffed to the brim with this very tobacco, a fitting center point to the vices that helped smooth out the edges of a rough day.

I close the humidor and keep the tin in my hand. A slight scraping noise announces my grasping a heavy crystal tumbler to the otherwise silent room. A deep popping sound soon accompanies it as I pull the cork from the patiently awaiting whisky bottle. I pour a generous dram into the glass, reveling in the glorious assault of complex scents grasping up at me. I gently place the bottle back next to my humidor and squeeze the cork back in, all the while enjoying the unabashedly strong smell of fine scotch.

Strong citrus tones meld with the fragrance of malt and honey in the air, intensifying as I breathe in closer to the rim of the glass. I close my eyes as the gap of nearly three decades is bridged within seconds. The once familiar and overlooked experience of a glass of whisky brings absolute empowerment to me now as I once again let my senses be enveloped. I sip gingerly, and am surprised at the smooth accessibility of the taste. I was expecting to be gagging and clawing at my throat like a toddler drinking mummy's brandy, but it goes down quite easily.

Somewhat sadly, I place the glass back down on the hutch and turn my attention back to the tin still clutched in my right hand. I know that this is flake tobacco, and that it might cause me some trouble in handling it after so many years. As I open the tin, a welcoming smell of chocolate, raisins and hay floats gently upwards, mixing with the potent fumes of my scotch. Such stimulant delight.

My mouth turns downwards as I regard the contents of the tin. A flake slice is a rectangular cut of pressed tobacco that you can either rip into ribbons to sprinkle in your pipe, or you can fold and stuff it as it is. You need a long, thin pipe bowl to properly accommodate an intact flake. Once again, my eyes turn to the hutch and take in the small collection of pipes sitting there. My gaze seems to rest on my old Turkish Meerschaum pipe, an old warrior tanned golden-brown from years of service. I remember almost exclusively using it when I was smoking Orlik due to its perfect proportions for that kind of tobacco.

With a deep exhale of nervous trepidation, I delicately reach for it and prepare to revisit an old ritual from which I am removed more than twenty years. I pick up a flake and hold it over the tin so any loose shreds will not be wasted as I progress. It creases along the length without protest, and I find myself smiling at how easy it is so far. I fold it again, end-to-end this time, and it begins to crumble slightly. I know that I must double it over once more so it will fit perfectly, but I seem to recall this part being rather difficult to pull off. With a steadying breath, I attempt the last step and it all begins to fall apart. Hastily and unceremoniously I stuff it into the pipe, hoping that I have left enough of an air-pocket down the bottom of the bowl for the tobacco to expand.

I carefully light the pipe with a long wooden match and make my way over to the couch, puffing gently between sips of heady scotch. I sit here for more than an hour, exploring the myriad of flavors gleaned from these two simple pursuits whilst lazily watching wispy tendrils of smoke swirl slowly towards the ceiling.

I understand again why I used to employ these methods to escape the unrelenting pressures of the outside world. I know that most people in my generation never bothered with these supposed old-man pursuits, chasing pre-mixed drinks and harder drugs to get their fix. The irony of the present situation certainly doesn't escape me, I am fully aware that the next time someone calls me an old man I will laugh a bit harder than usual.

After a measure of time, the soothing effects of this midnight pursuit lessen, and I am faced with the prospect of tomorrow. Audrey was, as I predicted, incredibly supportive of my leaving that haven of stress and misery. She reminded me that James had recently re-extended his offer of employment at his antiques store. She said the pay was not what I would have gotten at another management job, but I would not be as overworked there either.

There is a Chinese Proverb which states that those who know when they have enough are truly wealthy. This readily applies to my current situation, as I am again surrounded with a plethora of glorious things that I had thought lost to me forever. I have gleaned so much pleasure from the simple luxuries in regular abundance in this era, let alone the immense joy derived from re-uniting with the love of my life. If I can hold on to the profound satiation provided from such aspects of my life, I cannot see myself ever becoming complacent.

It saddens me that I always seemed to want more in these youthful years in which I am now reinhabiting, suffering though long, stressful hours each day so I could buy more things in my spare time. Said things quickly lost their value to me as the desire to go and purchase something new overtook me. Coming from my sad existence in the now-nonexistent future, where everything was within easy reach except for what mattered, has helped to drive home the absurd nature of consumerism.

If I can keep the lessons of my past as a check against renewed dissatisfaction, I believe I will be much happier working a lot less.

My job will not be my life this time, I vow.

We discussed the opportunity over dinner, her gently guiding me to taking the position, and I all too willing to be persuaded. I found the courage to call James, and then almost jumped out of my skin when he finally answered. His voice through the phone-line sounded exactly the same as when last we spoke in that enigmatic Mr. Montgomery's machine room. For a few moments I was dumb with fear, and James was getting rather agitated on the other end of the line.

After a few steadying breaths, the realization finally surfaced: Of course he would sound identical! His synthesized body was formed as an exact copy of James in his prime. This would be the era in which you would find the matching candidate, I am sure.

He exclaimed delight at my interest, and didn't ask a single question about how I came to be requesting this position. He said to come in tomorrow if I didn't mind, as he was really short of staff at present. Happy to feel wanted, I agreed without much hesitation.

Now, as I sit here with an empty glass and warmed pipe in hand, I cannot help but feel nervous about walking into the unknown for the first time since I have been back. I know that this decision will probably encompass my desire to live less stressfully, but I cannot know for certain. Up until I quit my job, I had been rediscovering things for better or worse, but now I will be embarking on the first really divergent course since my arrival. It scares me to some degree that I will no longer have my memory to guide me as a buffer against my past mistakes.

Tomorrow is the beginning of an entirely new set of possibilities and mistakes. I should be thankful, and for the most part I believe I am, but the unforgiving nature of the present world means that I am also rather anxious as well. I find myself planning tomorrow morning more carefully than I usually do, making sure I will not be late for my first day. Even though I am sure James would not be too hard on his closest friend for such an event, I do not want to give the impression of a poor employee and thusly a poor choice on his behalf.

I sit back and close my eyes. Having your life in your own hands is a sensation that is both enlivening and nerve-wracking. I relish having the freedom to choose, yet dread the outcomes of said choices. What an absolutely ridiculous state of mind, yet I am sure I am not alone in this way of thinking. I can think of plenty of people, my old self included, that are simply too afraid to make a change once they deem themselves secure enough in life, and suffer the misery of a sterile existence. If you are unlucky enough to have a life that has gone entirely to plan, I pity you. I really do.

For the hundredth time, I am grateful that Audrey is here to help me though this tangent life. Despite the fact that she doesn't know exactly what she is helping me overcome, I believe she is doing a wonderful job in being my anchor amidst these churning waters of change and possibility.

All I know for certain is that for the first time in a very long stretch, I am looking at the future as something worth experiencing.

Divergence

Specks of dust float gently in thin shards of light.

The air is musty and comforting, and I find myself constantly smiling in open contentment at such pleasing surrounds. My fingers absently trace the scratches and dents in the worn wooden counter I stand behind as my eyes struggle to absorb the thousand tiny details cluttered before them.

James nods as he regards me warmly. "You do look pleased, Alan. I simply cannot imagine you wearing that expression at your previous job. That is for certain."

"It is an interesting place," I note quietly, and am interrupted by a burst of laughter.

"Interesting?" James asks with a tilt of his head. "Well, I guess you could call it that if you're ninety five, and looking for a new gramophone to replace the old one. Maybe you could find one of those fandangled hands-free ones if you play your cards right."

I chuckle softly. "I don't know James; I think you may be looking at this the wrong way."

"How do you mean?"

"Well, one day things like these . . ." I say as I make a sweeping gesture around the room. "May be near-impossible to find. I think some people may share that opinion, and view a place like this as a treasure trove of last chance purchasing."

"Last chance purchasing?" replies James, an amused grin working its way across his features. "Hey, Alan . . . I should call the store Last Chance Purchasing."

"Only if you want to sound like a pretentious knob-jockey mate."

We laugh.

"So Alan, you all clear on how to run this place?"

"It is a comparatively easy job compared to my last: Mind the store, help customers out if they approach me, but don't pester them or do the hard sell. Try not to break shit."

"That's about it."

"Sounds great," I say, and genuinely mean it.

From the moment I nervously opened the chipped yellow door with "Sandra's Antiques and Treasures" garishly printed on its glass panel and stepped through into the store, a comforting feeling of curiosity and belonging washed over me. Within the unashamedly hodgepodge display that spans every wall lies a marvelous collection of antiquities from as far back as the Eighteenth Century. An early transistor radio sits next to some brass charcoal flat irons, and perched alongside them is a ruby-colored glass banquet lamp.

Monetary value seems to hold no sway here, as shown with the rather peculiar sight of a Victorian ivory manicure set draped carelessly on top of a scratched cedar voting box. This complacency affects a sort of nonchalant honesty about the store, as if a customer actually purchasing an item off the shelf is an entirely secondary motivation to the store's existence.

"Who is Sandra anyway?" I ask James as he is about to head out the door.

He turns distractedly and says, "Mate, I haven't got a clue. I haven't changed my name secretly if that is what you are asking. I own this place, have for some time now, but I never could bring myself to change that name. I have grown to like it, I believe."

"Yeah, it's certainly flamboyant," I say in amusement. "Good choice I think."

"Thanks mate. Gotta run." He smiles and opens the door. "Really happy you decided to join me here."

I stare at the empty space in which he was just standing, struggling to find the humorous side of the accidental revelation implied within his casual aside.

"I am too . . ." I mutter to the vintage chrome samovar that sits near the cash register.

I set about familiarizing myself with the mind-boggling size of the store's inventory. If James only knew how much this sort of thing sold for in my time he could have made an enormous profit. Then again . . . there had to be a supplier for that outrageous display at Mr. Montgomery's apartment. There was a lot I never asked James, and a lot he didn't want to be asked at that. Upon reflection, it is not a far stretch to imagine him working comfortably outside the blurry line of legality to get things moving along for himself.

I begin my explorations by approaching an Art Nuevo brass jardinière, and am disappointed to find it is covered in dust. As I continue to make my way around the store, I find that a lot of things here look coldly abandoned. I feel my eyebrows knit in confusion as I regard the apparent neglect surrounding me. How has this place been around for so long if nothing ever seems to move from the shelves? I search for some cleaning products so I can find a duster or a rag to give these poor antiques a bit of attention.

There is nothing around the counter, nor in the shelves behind it. I look around the store and see only one door besides the main entrance. It is a sturdy looking metal monstrosity that seems totally out of place within this decaying and dirty store. It certainly appears to be the most accessed and well-used part of this building, with no signs of dust on the floor below it. Well, if there is going to be a cloth somewhere, that would be it.

I quickly stride over and turn the handle. It resists with the kind of precise stiffness that indicates a well made lock. I step back in confusion. A storeroom? If the objects behind this door are considered valuable enough for a separate secure area, they must be precious indeed considering the ill-treated nature of the priceless collection in the main showroom. I begin to doubt whether there are even antiques stored behind that door at all. The shop in which I stand looks as though it has been untouched in many years, collecting dust in overlooked dejection while the locked door in front of me enjoys constant thoroughfare.

I slowly walk back to the front counter and mull over the peculiar nature of this strange store. I simply must ask James what is behind that door.

Or should I?

Perhaps I should just bring in a rag from home and spend my days ignoring the strange, unmarked door at the back of the store. I could probably manage that for a while, taking his money for my silence and treating this as an easy way to get money so Audrey and I can live comfortably.

It strikes me just how much my decision-making process has changed since my rebirth into this decadent timeline. Whereas before I would carefully prod through life like a disenfranchised turtle, examining each pebble that came across my path for signs of danger; I find myself throwing caution to the wind as I embrace the addictive qualities of insubordination.

Reality is what one makes of it. All my years have taught me little else. I could make a fuss and demand to know what is hidden away in plain sight, what this store is really used for . . . or I could accept the quiet understanding James is probably expecting me to reach and play along in his little game. I imagine he was rather pleased in having me employed at his "store", as he would have to weave less of an intricate story with such an old friend. In fact, no story need be woven at all.

The decision comes easily, fuelled by the desire to live a less restricted life this time around. I will allay my curiosity as both a favor to James, and ultimately to myself.

Still, this place is going to need a clean, no matter what.

I drink in the solitude that surrounds me as the clock slowly measures the passing of the day, finding that I am strangely at peace with the stifling stillness. I know it should probably be bothering me to be alone again after what my life had been comprised of before I came back, but this is a different kind of silence.

It is a sort of quiet optimism; a lull between moments of rich, saturated servings of life. A chance to take a deep breath and reflect on the amazing things you just accomplished, or indeed to look ahead at what may come. These moments of resolute solace feel essential to me in a life full of momentum and possibility. Whereas before I was busy putting the misery of my day-to-day life out of my mind, now I am happily lost just guessing what kind of surprises might be in store for me today.

The door opens for the first time since James left some hours ago, and a man in a grey flannel suit strides in. He certainly looks out of place in a dusty store named "Sandra's Antiques and Treasures." I smile and say hello. He looks at me with narrowed eyes.

"You Alan?" he demands, pulling a Lucky Strike cigarette from its packet and lighting it with a wooden match.

Can you even get that brand in Australia?

"Yes," I reply in a neutral tone, not entirely sure if I am in trouble or not. His expression melts into a friendly smile and he extends his hand.

"Roger Andrews," he states as we shake hands firmly. I take his appearance with something akin to trepidation. He is tall, lean and confident. His neatly trimmed short grey hair and tasteful gold jewelry remind me of nothing so much as a Hollywood gangster. His clean shaven, angled face does little to lessen this illusion.

"You already know who I am it seems," I say nervously.

"James told me his old mate was looking after the store, which is excellent news considering the trouble we had with Samantha."

"Who's that?"

"A fuck-up, that's all you need to know Alan." He is unable to hide the dark edge to his voice.

"Oh dear," I manage. Roger looks at me piercingly, and then he is suddenly grinning ear to ear again.

"What are you, eighty?" He laughs. "Oh dear indeed." He looks around the store briefly, before his eyes settle on the back door.

"Do you need anything?" I query politely.

"James around?" comes the distracted response. His gaze is now focused unwaveringly on the shiny metal anomaly at the back of the store.

"No, sorry. He didn't say if he would be coming back today," I respond in my best shopkeeper's voice. "I got the impression that he was not going to though."

"Ah . . ." His expression clouds over in a potent rage. I watch him struggle as he forces a smile onto his reddened features. The resulting sneer has such a sharp edge that I'm afraid he will bite his flimsy cigarette in twain. Finally he turns to regard me, still leering despite his best efforts. "Let him know he missed his appointment with Roger Andrews the next time you see him. He will know what you mean."

"Sure, not a worry," I respond, trying to inject as much cheery optimism into my voice as possible.

"Been a pleasure, Alan," he says flatly as he quickly exits the drab store, snuffing his cigarette out on a vintage porcelain ashtray.

Interesting first day. I think to myself wearily.

Sometime later, near the end of an otherwise uneventful shift, James returns to see if his shop has avoided being set aflame in my care. He looks flustered and busy, but manages to put on a smile for his old friend.

"Anything exciting happen mate?" he asks with a grin plastered over his features. I am unsure if he knows about my little visit, but I play the fool for him for the hundredth time.

"Well, maybe not exciting, but certainly memorable," I say, forcing a reflective tone.

He blinks, taken aback at the news that something actually happened in his quiet store. "Well . . . that is . . . good I guess. Unusual."

"Is it?"

"Yes," he says shortly, giving me a look that warns me not to continue down this path. I look at him for a moment, and then slowly nod in understanding. He visibly relaxes. "So what happened?"

"Roger Andrews is a funny sort of guy."

"Hmmm?" James says in confusion. "Did he come here?"

"Yes, he seemed to think you both were meeting for an appointment."

"Here?" he repeats, looking around the store as though the chipped chamber-pots and assorted walking sticks would spell out all the answers for him.

I nod, trying to suppress a grin.

"Hmmm . . . Alright. I'll get that squared right away."

"Who is that guy?"

"Oh . . . my boss I guess." He seems nervous. I cannot recall the last time I have seen him so. The promise I made to myself today to stay out of whatever mysterious plot James is hatching begins to feel strangely hard to keep at present.

"Alright . . ." I say, letting the many unanswered questions die on my lips for the moment. Despite my newly acquired disregard for social convention, I still find it hard to stand around and be lied to, especially by one who calls himself your closest friend.

I do believe he will come to me with the truth soon, yet I also acknowledge the fact that James does not enjoy verbal conflict (at least not yet), and there is a chance he will put off the revelation of his true occupation for quite some time.

"I almost forgot," he says distractedly as he fumbles around in his briefcase. I look on placidly as James produces a small porcelain elephant decorated with haphazard gold gilding. It rattles slightly as he hands it to me. "A gift for Audrey as thanks for her convincing you to come work for me. I know how much she loves elephants, and it would only gather dust here. The tackier the better right?"

"Thanks," I say with a look of confusion. "Are you sure?"

"No problems. Not many perks in owning an antiques store, but one advantage is being able to palm off useless crap as presents." I notice his usual easy-going manner is absent as he stumbles through this attempt at levity. His eyes dart around the room distractedly, and I can barely hear him speak. "I am sure she will like it."

"Sure," I manage to respond, still regarding him with a questioning eye. "I will pass on your regards."

James mutters his goodbyes and says I will see him tomorrow sometime as he rushes out the store. As the front door closes, he reminds me to turn off the lights and to make sure I flip the lock on the front door as I leave.

In the last few hours before I can close up and go home, I find myself regarding the locked metal door at the back of the store in open curiosity, wondering if I will ever find out what is hidden behind its plain exterior. I otherwise seem to be turning to face the entrance of the store to see what interesting character might be waltzing through the threshold next.

Strangers

What an odd day.

I have just finished my first shift at Sandra's Antiques and Treasures, and I am surprised to admit to myself that it has been quite the eventful introduction to this new vocation.

The faded yellow door is locked behind me, and I am standing contentedly at the entrance, peering about the street with a silly grin plastered all over my face. As far as first days go, this was about as interesting as they come.

My new job is essentially minding an abandoned store, which means I am free to pass the time each day pretty much how I see fit. A laptop and portable internet are essential here I think. Adding a hint of mystery to the whole caper is the fact that the only part of the store that seems to get used is off limits to me at present. I am apparently not allowed to acknowledge its existence, if James' behavior this afternoon is anything to go by.

All this adds up to a damn easy job with a slightly secretive side. Despite this shady element, I am certain to prefer this over the exhausting pool of stress that I was forced to bathe in before this opportunity arose.

I cannot help a feeling of satisfaction and contentment overtake me as I begin walking down the street to the bus stop. Sure, there may be an undercurrent of uncertainty slowly eroding my temporary satiation, but that is only apparent to me when I look hard enough for it.

The intricate tapestry of everyday life that those suffering from stress never seem to acknowledge shines brightly in a spectrum of loud color. A tea house accented with fresh royal blue paint, the skittering of autumn leaves past my feet, the smell of lavender from atop a window sill. The texture of the day is indeed rich when your senses allow it to be.

With notable disappointment at the speedy arrival at my destination, I sit down on the hard steel inside the bus stop shelter and begin waiting. The unexplored pleasures of the street jump at me from the edges of my vision, teasing me with unrelenting frequency.

It seems a shame to simply go home after such an eventful afternoon; to hide away from the world and wait for the following day for the next opportunity to interact with my newfound surrounds.

"Fuck it," I say to the tepid air around me as I stand up and move away from the empty bus shelter.

I try and suppress a smile worming across my features as I feed my wanderlust, wanting to appear at least slightly normal to the casual passerby.

O'Connell St welcomes me with casual indifference, spreading its open arms in a relaxed ease to accommodate another nameless traveler. I wander past twenty-four hour bakeries, fashion outlets, gourmet burger joints and expensive delicatessens with equal reverence before stopping dead in my tracks in front of the regal façade of the Oxford Hotel. I remember spending many an hour trapped within the Banque wine bar with my old employers, pretending to exude class as we requested French champagne from the blank-eyed bartenders.

Something tugs from my subconscious, compelling me to enter the building and place an order. Far from rebelling against my mental urgings, I willingly accede to my minds directions and enter the white, modern interior.

The minimalist décor somewhat offends me. It is as though someone came into the apartment from my past, slammed down a glass vase and brass mirror and called it stylish. The grey marble bar randomly accented with glass only serves to confirm that the juxtaposition of modernity and baroque has been completely botched.

Shaking my head at the butchery of timeless design for the sake of being supposedly cutting-edge, I make my way over to the bar.

"Hello," says a silky smooth voice from behind the marble monstrosity. She sounds bored and disenfranchised.

"Howdy," I respond automatically before I even bother looking at her. It seems I cannot take my eyes off the soapy marble bar.

"What can I get you?" she asks in a tone that suggests more than the common interpretation. I look up and my breath catches in my throat.

She is beautiful. Icy blue eyes regard me with a bemused expression as her pale blonde eyebrows arch playfully in patient understanding. Thin lips flirt with a smile, as she drums her fingers on the bar. Her hair is pulled back in a tight ponytail, and I have to stop myself from studying the lithe form beneath her black shirt.

"Gibson. Up," I manage. "You have Hendricks?"

She shakes her head with a smile, then says, "No such luck I am afraid,"

"Okay."

"You desperate for Scottish gin?" she asks, wearing a bemused, yet intrigued expression on her face.

"If possible."

"We have Bombay," she offers.

"Sure thing," I concede. "Don't they have name-tags here?"

She laughs softly at my clumsy attempt to glean her name. "Nope."

"Oh . . . right."

"Vera," she responds with a slow smile. "You have me at a disadvantage."

"Alan," I gush, and then straighten my back to try and compose myself.

"Well, Alan . . ." Vera continues, "Bombay Gibson Martini?"

"Please."

Vera nods, and moves to the back wall to mix my drink. I try and look nonchalant by peering about the room and studying its bland features to pass the time. Vera returns with my drink.

"Make it six dollars," she says with a wink. I am not sure if this is cheap, but I assume it is considering her body language.

"Thanks Vera," I manage as I produce the requisite gold coins. I give her an awkward nod and start to move off.

"Listen, Alan," she begins as she looks around the empty bar. "I have my break coming up. Do you mind if I share a drink with you?"

Were women always this forward? I think to myself as an embarrassed blush works its way into my features. Loyalty to Audrey surges from within to frequently nip at my conscious thoughts, but I manage to convince myself that nothing untoward will happen. Secretly, I am very flattered at the attention that I don't honestly believe I deserve.

"Sure," I respond after a few long seconds.

"Take a seat." She smiles, confident in her undeniable beauty. "I will join you in a few minutes."

I make my way over to the black leather booth seat nearest to the bar and sit down unceremoniously. Feelings of uncertainty slither around my body, causing me to shudder with every sporadic mental protest. What am I doing? It isn't like me at all to plant the seeds of what could end up growing into a very awkward situation.

I consider simply getting up and walking out the door, disappointing Vera and saving myself some embarrassing admonitions; but I cannot bring myself to stand up and go through with my plan.

"Hey there," Vera says happily as she sits across from me at my table. "You haven't touched your drink. Something wrong?"

"Oh . . ." I respond clumsily. "No, just forgot."

"What could make a man forget about his drink?" She asks coyly. I pause for a moment in awe of her presence. She smells of vanilla and cloves, a delicate scent that unfolds slowly as the seconds pass us by. It is as though she is a construct of distilled ideals, rather than a mere human being. It is not a base attraction that I feel for her, not the primal and insatiable lust that I feel for Audrey. It is the sickly mix of reverence and trepidation that comes from beholding something alien and beautiful.

"Indeed . . ." I raise the cool glass to my lips and take a hearty gulp. "Cheers."

"Cheers." Vera laughs softly at my lack of protocol. "You are an odd sort."

"How so?"

"It's just that you seem to have refined tastes without the snobby attitude. It is rare."

"I guess you would get all sorts coming through those doors," I say as diplomatically as I can.

"You have no idea . . ." she says as she stretches out luxuriously like a cat in warm sunlight. "It is amazing how most people who pretend as though they are classy enough to belong in a fancy place such as this are really just boorish and pedestrian."

"I know what you mean," I say, though I am not sure I actually do.

"But people like you are rare," she repeats intensely, a harsh edge to her voice. "What is a genuine man doing in a morgue like this?"

I laugh nervously. "What do you mean?"

"Fishing for compliments?" Vera asks with a slow smile.

"Not really. I am honestly not sure of your meaning." I take a small sip from the heavy martini glass, but the taste hardly registers on my tongue.

"You don't belong here," comes her gentle response.

"Not really, I guess. Just revisiting some memories."

"Ahh . . ." she says in a quiet understanding. "That makes more sense."

I look at her with narrowed eyes, and then finish my drink. "And you thought *I* was different . . ."

Vera laughs, blushing slightly at my questioning gaze. "You're right, I'm sorry for coming across a bit strange."

I nod my head and watch as she slowly drinks her bottle of Cooper's Pale Ale. "So how do you like working here?" I ask, attempting to change the subject.

"Are you kidding?" she says in a flustered tone. "I hate it."

"Why?"

"Despite the obvious?" she asks as she waves her arm at the surrounding room. So it is not just me who thinks this bar looks like a hastily decorated hospital ward. "Nobody seems to want to be themselves here, I guess. Everyone acts as though they are playing a part someone else wrote for them."

"Isn't that the case with most bars?" I ask her with a chuckle.

"Could be. I'm not sure. This is the first one I've worked at."

"I don't know, Vera." I am studying her in open curiosity. "People like to pretend they are someone else in these sorts of places."

"What about you then Alan?" she asks, showing more than just casual interest in my response. I feel myself shifting uncomfortably in my seat under the intensity of her icy blue gaze. "Are you pretending?"

"I am too old for that sort of thing," I respond before I realize what I am saying. Vera looks surprised for a few seconds before she bursts out laughing.

"So how old are you then?"

"Almost sixty five," I respond, trying to sound light-hearted and probably failing miserably in the process.

"You don't look a day over fifty," she jokes, reaching out to take my hand. "Let's get out of here Alan."

"What about the rest of your shift?" I ask with a slight stutter, quite obviously taken aback at her suggestion.

"I was going to quit soon . . ." Vera pauses in brief reflection. "It will probably be getting unbearably quiet around here soon anyway."

I look at her hesitantly, too polite to pull my hand away, but craving desperately to do so. Despite her smooth charms and alluring confidence, I suddenly get the overwhelming feeling that I am being chatted-up by little more than a child. Her simplistic view of the world is so unlike my own that she almost comes across as a caricature. Despite her impossible beauty, Vera is beginning to look flat and one dimensional. The vessel of an ideal without the soul to inhibit it.

"Nothing is ever that simple," I say, almost to myself.

"Sure it is," Vera soothes. "Let's go somewhere completely new. Let our imaginations weave a new path."

I stare at her, slowly shaking my head at her naivety. I squeeze her hand in sympathy, and she takes this as confirmation of her desires.

"What are we waiting for then?"

My phone rings, cutting through the silence that was slowly drawing a curtain between us. I gently pull my hand back as I tell Vera, "I should get that."

"Hey love," Audrey's voice comes through the tinny earpiece. "How was your first day at the store?"

"Not bad honey," I respond in the sort of casually affectionate tone you can only use with your partner. A look of understanding crosses Vera's features. She stands up slowly, setting her beer down with a careful grace. Rather than the expected display of anger or annoyance, I am surprised to see a brief shadow of sympathy fall across her features. In what seems to be the persistent normality of my reawakened life, I am almost certain as to Vera knowing much more than she is letting me know.

"A woman's instinct I suppose, knowing the exact moment to call you . . ." she whispers sadly, her eyes searching my own for an answer to her unuttered questions. "I hope she takes care of you Alan."

A Decision

The road stretches far into the distance.

Warm sunlight filters through my car's windscreen, inducing Audrey into a serene slumber. My lips part in a soft smile at the sight of her sleeping head bobbing to the rhythm of the undulated surface beneath us. I take in the serene beauty of the South Australian countryside as I drive.

Sturdy eucalyptus trees dot rolling fields of bright yellow Canola flowers, divided with rusted barbed wire fencing threaded loosely through coarse wooden stumps. A few minutes travel and the bright flora gives way to plains of dead weeds and muted green grass upon which sheep, cows and horses lazily feed, depending upon on which property you pass. Ramshackle tin sheds perch next to modern houses, and smooth bitumen roads meet with worn dirt tracks seemingly at random. We occasionally pass another car, the loud whoosh it makes as it speeds past my windshield making me temporarily more alert.

The blue-grey veil of autumn clouds covers the landscape, begrudgingly allowing small shards of sunlight though to illuminate random spots of the scenery around us: An old tractor, a collapsed rainwater tank, a large rock with graffiti scrawled upon it perched defiantly near the side of the road. It occurs to me that the Australian outback is not a pretentious, movie style collective of exquisitely neat fields grouped obligingly near dead straight roads, with bright red farmhouses welcoming weary travelers. It is more beautiful than that. It is functional, yet whimsical; random, yet strangely efficient. It is a wonderful paradox of toughness and vulnerability. A harsh environment with a gentle facade.

I spot a large, black circle of scorched earth in the center of a field. Bright shoots of verdant green poke though the destruction; much healthier than the surrounding dull grass that was not lucky enough to burn. It brings to mind something a teacher once told me in primary school: A bushfire is a chance for a forest to renew. They rely on them to stay strong and fresh, ridding the forest of unwanted growth and allowing the larger trees room to grow once more.

Cleansing by fire.

It struck me then, as it does now as a rather cruel incarnation of natural selection. Of course, humanity does much the same with bullets and borders.

I push such melancholy from my thoughts and feel the soothing effect of solitude wash over me once more, allowing the steady thrum of the motor and vibrations from the road we traverse to ease my tensions.

As we pass a small pokey vineyard, I recall Audrey chatting amiably about how she used to go grape-picking when she was a girl. She would follow her parents out to a vine, get a bunch of grapes, then sneak back into the warmth of their car and eat plump ovals of freshly picked Merlot until she fell asleep.

We are driving down these lonely roads because of her. She mentioned last night as we sat down for dinner, that now that I had more time to spare we could go visit her parents for the weekend. I was originally hesitant, not wanting to spend my second weekend back sitting at the kitchen table of their farmhouse discussing the cattle over rock-hard scones and bitter tea.

I relented when I realized just how much she missed them, and how long it had apparently been since I have had the time take her down to stay. I let her convince me that the country air would do me good, though honestly I said yes just to lessen the guilt of the previous afternoon's bizarre events upon my conscience. Despite the fact that I didn't do wrong by Audrey, I felt that I should somehow make it up to her for simply getting myself into that situation.

That and the smile that I got when I agreed with her idea brightened up the room for hours. I steal another look at her gorgeous slumbering face as I drive onwards, getting ever closer to her parents house as the minutes drag by.

The slow crunch of gravel from under heavy tires and the high-pitched squeal of warm brakes announce our arrival at their doorstep before our car even comes into view. A long trail of dust from behind our car slowly settles as I gently shake Audrey's shoulder and whisper at her to wake up. She blinks lethargically, yawning in response to the intrusion, then grins and sits upright, looking in open contentment at her old home. It is quite a nice place to look at; a Victorian house that has weathered the harsh elements with good grace. White painted walls, slightly chipped, and a green tin roof with four brick chimneys thrusting through to greet the sky.

I see Martin, Audrey's father is already opening the front door to come greet us. He is a heavy-set, sturdy man in his mid sixties. Deep lines around his eyes mark well a lifetime spent in the harsh Australian sun, yet his posture betrays no meek subservience to his age. His short-cropped grey hair still has strands of brown near the temples, as if proclaiming to all who care to look that he still has some youth in him yet. Yellowed teeth announce an easy smile as he approaches our car, walking purposefully to the passenger door. I notice he is dressed as he always did, blue denim shirt and tan moleskin trousers.

"Daddy!" Audrey exclaims happily. "I am no invalid. You don't need to help me out of the car."

"Dearest, there is nothing wrong with being a gentleman." He chuckles warmly at her, and then gives me a curt nod. "Alan."

"Hi Martin," I respond, attempting a friendly tone.

"Humph," he mutters, turning towards the house with Audrey by his side. She gives me an apologetic look as she follows him in. I take my time opening the boot and getting our luggage, not in any particular rush to go and join them. I seem to get the same treatment each time we visit, something akin to an interloper whom he has being ordered to tolerate. It has never been revealed to me if I did something particularly distasteful to him, or if all of Audrey's previous partners got the same love-less embrace.

"Alan, dear," says someone from the porch. "Has that old grouch started with you already?"

I turn my head to see Audrey's mother Laura standing at the front door, hands on her hips and slowly shaking her head. She has aged far less gracefully than her husband, her frail frame bent with age, skin wrinkled and slightly sagging. She is only a few years older than Martin, but time has been less friendly to her. Of course, she is far kinder and more respectful to me than her more upright partner, so looks can conceal many truths as usual. In the movies, the uglier a character the meaner their disposition, but out here in the world of three dimensions that is not always the case.

"Well, you could say so," I reply wearily. "I would be lying if I said I wasn't expecting it though."

"He is not going to change his ways this late in the game," Laura states bitterly, not bothering to conceal the tinge of sadness to her voice. "Come inside, then. Let's get that luggage put away."

I follow her inside, taking care not to bump into any of the numerous side tables littered with porcelain mice and glass cats. She opens the door to the guest room, and I manage to suppress a violent cough caused by the swirls of dust floating before me; no doubt disturbed by the first sign of movement the room has seen in some time. I wait until she has left the room to open the window as wide as I can.

"Wow, talk about abandoned," Audrey mutters as she joins me minutes later. "Either filth gathers here at an alarming rate, or they simply don't come in here at all."

"It's odd."

"I know."

"Hmmm," I respond, not really wanting to broadcast the many acidic comments wending their way around my thoughts like a hungry shark.

"Anyway," Audrey says as she gives me a firm hug, "let's head over to the kitchen, Mum has broken out the scones."

"Already?"

"Yep," she giggles. "Oh come on, they aren't that bad are they?"

"They smell like piss," I whisper. "And they are as unyielding as your father."

"He is a bit of a pain," she admits grudgingly. "Just keep your chin up and don't act offended when he baits you, 'cause he will pounce at the first sign of weakness. I think it is all just a game to him."

I grin. "Can I play too?"

"I . . . don't think this is your area of expertise." She laughs good-naturedly. "Just let him have his fun, and I will make it up to you later."

'Bribing me with sex.' I shake my head, looking at the dusty bed in open derision. "I just don't know if that'll work in this house."

"Come on," she says impatiently as she leads me out the room. We wend our way back through the overly decorated house, emerging into the hot kitchen. I inwardly sigh as I catch Martin grumpily regarding me over the rim of his coffee mug. He is sitting at their polished dinner table, back as straight as a flag pole, with his free hand resting comfortably on a red napkin.

"Settle in ok?" Laura asks in a warm voice, attempting to divert my attention from her domineering husband.

"Yes, thank you Laura," I respond politely. She nods to me and turns back to the spotlessly clean oven, rubbing her hands in its warmth while she keeps an eye on the clock.

"How have you been Daddy?" Audrey asks her father as she pulls up a chair next to him. His expression brightens as his beloved daughter addresses him, and he gives a happy nod. I clumsily sit down across from her, picking up a pastel blue coaster and turning it in my hands anxiously.

"Well enough darling, well enough," Martin responds, as if by admitting to being happy he would be less of a man. He shifts in his chair uncomfortably and changes the subject. "We've had some unexpected arrivals at the pasture lately though."

"Martin, leave it," Laura scolds from her vigil. "Wait until after we have had our meal before you start that business."

He gives her a sharp glare, but begrudgingly accedes to her request. I find myself examining the kitchen thoroughly in an attempt to avoid his haughty gaze. Unlike the impossibly dusty guest room, every surface here is fastidiously clean and tidy. Stainless steel appliances are polished in a glaring sheen, unlike the usual fingerprint-covered mess that you find in most households. The countertops are without a single crumb, and I am half-expecting a 1950's style commercial to break in the room out while I am not looking.

The room is so far detached from everyday life that it gives the impression that nobody would actually cook here, but I know from my previous visits that this is not the case.

I guess that cooking is one of the only thing Martin lets his wife devote any amount of time to, and as such she spends an inordinate amount of time hovering around here before and after each meal, scrubbing and polishing in a vacant glide.

"Ah, they should be ready now," Laura mutters at the clock-face as she opens the oven door and produces her infamous scones; the enigmas that openly defy the lifetime of cooking expertise that Laura should probably possess.

"Good, good," Martin says, surprisingly content with the fact that he will soon be breaking his dentures on those rocks. He hurriedly drains the remaining coffee from his mug and knits his fingers together in anticipation.

"Here we go," Laura says proudly as she tips the hot scones into an awaiting woven basket on the tabletop. Steam rises in protest from the baked monstrosities as she walks back to the sink and deposits her tray there. A toasty, charred aroma drifts gently towards me, but it is quickly drowned in an invasively acrid scent of urine emanating from within the misshapen lumps of dough.

"They look yummy," Audrey says sweetly as she gives me a sly look.

"Dig in Alan," Martin instructs as he grabs a piping hot scone and takes a large bite. I should mention that this family enjoys their baked goods without the merciful support of jam or cream. "Well? Tuck in boy, we have some work to do shortly."

My lips manage to weakly smile in acquiescence as I reach for the basket. As I heroically chew my afternoon treat and nod pleasantly along with the banal kitchen chatter, I cannot help but wonder what chore Martin is going to unload on me this time.

***

"You know how to use this, Alan?" sneers Martin as he holds up a .308 Winchester rifle.

"I do, yes," I reply. "Isn't that a little over the top for a Dingo? A .22 should be fine."

"A pea shooter?" he barks. "Don't be such a girl. We are here to kill these pests, not to tickle them."

"How many calves have been killed?" I query in quiet submission. We are standing in his Den, in front of a heavy gun safe bolted securely to the floor.

"One so far, but that is enough to get me mad as hell."

"Daddy . . ." Audrey begins. "Do we have to go killing Dingoes while Alan is down? Can't you wait until we have gone back home to start firing your bullets into the bush?"

"Nonsense, these bastards will be back for more each night unless we put a stop to them. Alan is no baby; learning to hunt will do him a world of good."

"Well, I am not taking part," she says, a great deal of anger lacing her words. "I am sure Mum would much prefer I kept her company rather than getting blood over my clothes."

"I got spare clothes . . ." he says, but she is already storming out the room. "Humph . . . Looks like it is just you and me Alan."

"Great," I say unenthusiastically. "Are you going to pick up a gun as well, or is this just an exhibition?"

"Keep your shirt on boy." Martin swears tersely. "I'm getting there."

We make our way outside, avoiding passing the kitchen window where Audrey and Laura are most certainly armed with their disapproving looks, ready to slowly shake their heads at our slow trudge towards bloodshed. I follow Martin's determined, yet unhurried gait past the house and towards his pasture. The rifle I nervously hold seems awkwardly heavy. I cannot seem to find a way to hold it without feeling like awkward and foolish. I hear a Kookaburra laughing at my clumsy progress, and I scowl as I hear his friends readily joining in from the surrounding branches above me. Other birds quietly chirp in annoyance at their peaceful afternoon perch being interrupted by these jeering feathered ruffians.

Martin walks on unceasingly, seemingly more determined than before to reach his destination. We pass through a landscape of pale grass, dead Eucalypt leaves and the occasional nonchalant cow before he stops suddenly. I instinctively know we have arrived at our destination. He looks back at me with a smug expression on his face.

"I thought this might do the trick," he whispers menacingly.

"What?" I answer, uninterested in his spittle-infused barbarity.

"Use your damn eyes Alan," he scolds, pointing to a spot on the ground a little distance away.

"You really need to wake up."

I follow his arm to where a dingo lies trapped next to a fence post, its leg caught in what looks like a small bear trap, sans the vicious spikes that accompany the traditional device.

"What is that it's caught in?" I ask hesitantly, peering with narrowed eyes at this trapped creature before us.

"Dingo trap, you dolt," he mutters offhandedly. "Not always effective in an amateur's hands mind you . . . people just don't know where to put 'em."

"Yes," I reply. "Congratulations, then."

"Shut up, smart ass." He looks at me with fury made manifest. "This bugger shouldn't be here, he has upset the natural balance. He's a long way from home and isn't welcome. I'm sure you can manage to forgive my excitement at his demise."

I look at him in a mix of supplication and barely concealed disgust; the unsettling anticipation in his eyes neatly offsetting my feigned calm, and I find myself backing away from the imminent slaughter.

"Right then," I say meekly. "This hunt looks to be going easier than expected. Why don't you finish him off and we can head back?"

The sight of a grin slowly infusing his angered expression puts me ill at ease. He slowly shakes his head from side to side while his eager eyes unceasingly bore into my nervous gaze.

"No."

"I'm sorry?" I stammer.

"Alan, you need to do this yourself."

"What?" comes my shaky response. "You want me to kill this poor animal?"

"It is trapped," Martin says in a surprisingly gentle tone. "Walking away will only grant it a drawn out and painful death."

"Why don't you do it then?" I plea, not at all under-standing his sudden sadism.

"Alan . . ." Martin soothes, sounding detached and placating. "This is something you have to do yourself."

"Why?"

Martin looks at me, all traces of snide anger evapo-rated. I see a wisdom and understanding that seems to defy his personality thus far. He slowly closes his eyes and lets out a measured breath.

"Alan . . . show me your true self. Do you have the for-titude to do what is right and merciful, or do you want to simply coast through life avoiding hard decisions?"

"What do you know about hard decisions?" I blurt defensively.

"More than you will ever know." Martin sighs, look-ing deflated and weathered. "Put it out of its misery Alan. It is approaching its end no matter what. Be strong, and kill it before it starts to really suffer."

I look at the animal before us. It is strangely calm, re-garding us with slight curiosity peppered with casual in-difference. It seems to be ignoring the dried blood caked around its trapped hind leg, defying the logical onset of panic that should be gripping it in a claustrophobic embrace.

This moves me more than any display of aggressive panic ever could.

Here is a creature seemingly oblivious to its soon to be painful ascension from mortality. This is an oppor-tunity, right now, to prevent the commencement of pro-longed suffering. A true act of mercy delivered before this predator can come to terms with the inevitability of the situation.

I grip the rifle.

"That's right Alan," Martin says, guiding me gently with his weathered voice. "Go now."

I bring the dingo's head into my sights and steady my aim. The gun rises and falls with every slow breath I take, the muted sunlight glinting off the metallic barrel as I steady my body in anticipation of the oncoming recoil.

The trigger depresses effortlessly and the air cracks with the rifle's bold report. I close my eyes as the stock slams into my shoulder in response to the bullet exploding from the chamber . . .

"Alan," Martin says gently, sounding in that moment more like Mr. Montgomery than Audrey's father. "You did the right thing just now."

I feel an immense sadness grip me, an unrelenting pneumatic arm of rusted steel squeezing all optimism from my already frail psyche, methodically draining the fuel of life from previously hidden reserves deep within me. I feel numbness spread over me like an insipid fog, seeping into each pore with studied precision as I fight relentlessly to feel even the smallest sensation. Once sturdy walls crumble at a searching touch, turning to gritty sand that piles ever steadily at my immobile feet. Tears should well purposefully at my dried eyes, but even that small release is denied to me by this sudden oppressive specter that cloaks my soul.

This death, this apparition of consequence made tangible, cuts its way past my mental defenses in an unexpected assault of unstoppable prowess. It is as if a thread between this world and my mind has been violently severed, and I cannot say with certainty that I shall ever be the same again. We are defined and shaped by seemingly small actions entrenching themselves in our minds, becoming immovable and inexorable without our noticing.

Without a doubt this is such a moment.

I look searchingly around me, soaking in every detail imaginable without consciously acknowledging even the simplest observation. I blink rapidly and try to regain my bearings, seeking to impose rhythm on my erratic breathing. I do not know what to think, how to feel . . .

All I can say with absolute certainty is that the world feels colder.

Conflict

The air smells of sweat and cheap perfume.

"Having a good night?" yells a scantily dressed woman perched at the front bar. Her red high-heels claw into the chrome rail at her feet, mercifully anchoring her drunken swaying. I nod and smile half-heartedly as I grab my drinks and execute a calculated, swift retreat.

As I make my way back to our table, I find myself cringing at the intrusively loud music pumping through the numerous distorted speakers that litter the ceilings like oversized cobwebs. I shake my head in disappointment at the crass and constructed stimuli that suburbia provides when compared to the tranquil honesty of the outback from that we have just returned from.

Audrey, that mysterious social chameleon, decided it would be a great idea to catch up with James on our first night back from that disquieting visit to her parent's farm. Apparently she felt I needed distraction from that "Nasty Business" of Martin and his calf, and I can't fault her logic at that. James seemed aloof and distracted at first when I called to invite him, but he leapt at the notion of heading out to a crowded club when Audrey suggested it to me in a purposefully loud voice while we were conversing.

Cunning fox.

"There he is," James slurs as I sit down next to Audrey at our cramped little table. She gazes at me with flushed cheeks and heavy eyelids, broadcasting her inebriated state to any who would care to look, and gives my hand a not-so-gentle squeeze.

"We thought you were dead," she says with a mock serious expression on her face, a quivering grin fighting its way into the corners of her mouth. They both burst into fits of unrestrained mirth, Audrey leading the way in high pitched staccato squeals and James providing a backup chorus of bloated chuckles. I join in, bemused and gladdened to see them both transcended from every-day banality with the express permission and guidance from old Uncle Alcohol.

"You gonna sit there all day like a constipated monk?" James sloppily chastises me. "Or are you going to finally join us in celebrating . . . something."

"What should we celebrate?" Audrey asks excitedly, already beginning to slur her words.

"Drinks finally arriving on our table after such a long wait!" James responds giddily, leering at me with a thirsty glare.

The thick and heavy scent of an overcrowded club dances around my nostrils as I take a deep breath of supplication. Polished wood wet with beer, bodily fluids gathered between the creases of dark leather, and the cloying cloud of clashing synthetic scents that battle each other loudly out of sight.

"I have been taking it a bit slow, haven't I?" I admit begrudgingly.

"Yes!" Audrey and James yell almost simultaneously. Audrey shakes her head at me playfully, and then quickly gulps down the rest of her Baileys.

"We didn't do a toast," James pouts.

Audrey burps as she raises her empty glass. "Cheers."

"Good enough for me," James mutters and drains his Mojito.

Right. I think to myself. *Let's see what I am missing out on . . .*

I quickly struggle through two shots of green Chartreuse, and shudder in content as I feel their warmth imbue me. Before long I have joined them up on their lofty plateau of hedonistic flippancy, and together we bask in a soothing aura fuelled with simplistic comradery.

This is the first time I have been drunk in a long time . . . a really long time. It feels liberating to have the freedom to break the chains of the often oppressive and weighty constraints of sober thoughts. I look at the tacky pulsating colored lights that bathe the dance floor in a swathe of hypnotic pointlessness and find myself unwillingly entranced.

At every flicker of the numerous lights, as the colors swirl from green to red to blue to pink; I seem to lose my grip on reality and plunge deep into the black morass of my awaiting subconscious. Flimsy and diluted speculations, once banished with conscious rejection resurface as stalwart truths in this trance of mental acceptance. I begin to wonder if this future I am supposedly from exists only in my imagination. What if this previously accepted tale of time travel and second chances is a form of deluded fantasy? A self imposed confidence trick conjured up in the depths of my mind . . .

At once I hear my sensible self bark out reprimand to my wandering psyche, touting the impossibility of a near thirty year chimera. These thoughts echo quietly in the distance as my present thoughts refuse to accept logic as their rudder through this swirling eddy.

How can I properly determine that the last three decades of my life, before the jump back to this time-line, are not merely fragmented fiction dressed up in the comforting clothes of memory? Can I remember each day clearly, or are there only a few crisp recollections floating amidst the foggy haze of my own past?

Maybe I strung together a series of dreams to form this fantasy, culminating in a potent nightmare that kick-started my neglected senses? At this moment even that absurdity has the same validity as anything else I can conjure up in this ponderous state.

A voice from deep within the shadows of my mind quietly enquires as to why I am trying to cheapen everything by second guessing what I know to be true. Yet the louder, more fluid voices emboldened by this brief foray outside their mental cage pronounce fantastical facts with booming certainty and I close my eyes in defeated confusion.

"Alan . . ." James asks from across the table. "You had too much to drink?"

"Nah . . ." I croak when I remember how to move my lips. "I am just zoned out."

"Yep," he snorts. "That's pretty much the point of all that Chartreuse ingestion though, isn't it?"

"Yeah, I reckon so."

"How can you boys drink that stuff without gagging?" Audrey slurs as she rips the edges off a paper coaster.

"We got man parts. They act as a secret alcohol sponge," James blurts, and we all laugh together. The sharp sound acts as a mental anchor, pulling me back to reality as I look around with newly focused eyes.

"So . . . who was minding the store while we were away?" asks Audrey in a mildly curious tone. "Thanks again for letting Alan take Monday off as well as the weekend. You're a cool boss."

"Yeah . . . definitely not a jerk-face like my previous one," I agree readily. "But how did you manage to turn back the flood of customers angrily tearing down your shop's walls at the sudden and extended disappearance of my winning smile?"

"Hah! You mean your seedy salesman leer?" he retorts good-naturedly. "I assure you if we *had* any customers they would have been more relaxed without your high pressure tactics compelling them to buy a new antique valise."

"Hmm . . . If only we actually had a customer to try out those supposed skills on . . ."

"Yeah." He shrugs noncommittally. "Sometimes we are busy, sometimes not. Antiques don't sell like today's crappy electronic gadgets, but they sure do last longer."

"Were you behind the counter for a change?" Audrey asks with a grin. "I can't imagine that, no matter how hard I try."

"Nah . . . I just closed up for three days," he says as he waves her questioning stare away. "No big deal, it wasn't a busy week."

"I . . . thought you desperately needed staff?" I query hesitantly.

"I do. Sort of. It would be nice to have you working with me."

"Selling antiques, you mean?"

"Well, that would be nice as well," he responds. I see that his drunkenness relaxing his usually deflective persona. "I run private sales from that store mostly, but we can delve into that a bit later. I would certainly welcome someone buying *any* of that old crap off the shelves, but that is not how I make my money."

"What am I getting myself into here James?" I ask, suddenly not feeling as cheerful as before. Audrey's eyes bore into James' with intensity, but I cannot tell if she is angry or intensely curious.

"Look, it's no big deal," he soothes. "I am not some sort of hoodlum drug dealer or something. I facilitate sales for . . . antiques that are hard to come by via the usual channels. I am still a dealer in things that are old, just not the worthless junk I have on the displays there."

"James . . ." I respond with a degree of incredulity. "Some of the stuff gathering dust on those shelves are high-ticket items."

"Not compared to what I have for private buyers mate."

"Ohhh . . ." Audrey says, effortlessly placated with the echoes of criminality that James is admitting to. "That sounds sort of cool. Can we see one of your 'private' antiques?"

James grins slowly. "You wanna see my privates?"

Audrey and I groan simultaneously at his vulgar pun, but we cannot help but laugh.

"Err . . ." I say. "Better keep your pants on in such a public place."

"Fine, fine . . ." he says as he pretends to sulk. "Look, we can get into all of this later. I trust you Alan, and I would like to have you helping me out. For now I just need you to look innocent and take Joe Citizen's money if he is stupid enough to want to purchase any of my showroom stock."

"Innocent?"

"Poor choice of words," he soothes drunkenly. "It's not . . . well, legal, what I do . . . but it isn't evil, and it doesn't hurt anyone. I am absolutely certain of that."

Rather than be nervous or off-put about the confirmation that James works outside the law in the present like he did in my past, I am surprised to find myself rather intrigued at the notion. Somehow, I get the feeling that new doors are opening to an entirely different set of possibilities for my future. Every step I take that is different from my previous life seems to be the right one to take.

"This is all very exciting . . ." Audrey says suddenly. "However, I think I need to go and puke for a while. Don't mind me. Keep talking your smooth criminal talk. I'll be back."

"You ok?" I ask, regarding her with concern. She waves away my concern as she hastens to the bathroom on shaky legs.

"Just drunk."

We laugh quietly and consider switching to water ourselves. I look around the room and try my hardest to bring objects into focus with widened eyes, as if by willpower alone I can summon sobriety.

"James . . ." says a sharp voice from behind me. "I have been looking for you. Alan was it? Hello to you too."

Before I can turn around to see who our new visitor is, I notice the comfortably numb expression on James' face seize up in unmitigated panic.

"Roger," he stammers. "What brings you here? I didn't think you were the clubbing sort."

"You, James," he replies in a light-hearted tone laced with icy resolve. "You bring me here. Why else would you find someone like me in a hovel like this?"

"I . . . don't know," James replies in a defeated slump. I begin to feel a cold panic slowly spread from the pit of my stomach. Something is definitely wrong here.

"Of course you don't," Roger sneers. "Listen James . . . we need to have a little chat. If you could accompany me to the car park for a few minutes, then we can sort this misunderstanding out."

"What? Now?" he protests weakly, fear coating his tongue in a thick film of clumsiness.

"Yes," comes the monotone response. "You too Alan. Hurry up, I need a smoke."

I simply nod and attempt to stop my hands from shaking. I fervently hope that Audrey's appointment with the bathroom floor lasts as long as she thought it would.

"Up," barks a heavy set man in an ill-fitting suit from behind Roger's shoulder. James extends an apologetic glance my way as we both slowly rise to our feet. We are led at an unhurried pace out the front door and around the back of the club to a dimly lit, rain soaked car park. Trash is gathered in small, soggy piles inside the potholes that scar the bitumen, and the air smells of pungent rot.

"Is this really the way you want to do business Roger?" James asks in an incredulous tone. "With goons in dramatically lit car parks?"

"Smart mouth James," Roger replies angrily. "Honestly, I wouldn't mind that cheeky streak if you deigned to answer my calls, or opened your shop for me when I ask. As it is, even looking it you makes me upset . . . so *don't* push your luck with that poor excuse for bravado."

"Roger," he murmurs, all traces of confidence scattered like fine ash in a stiff breeze. "I am sorry I have avoided you this past week. I really am. It's just that what you paid for hasn't arrived yet, and I am not good at letting people down gently. I don't have tact."

"What a load of bullshit!" he yells menacingly. "Tact? This is not about manners! This issue has stemmed from the simple fact that you have failed to deliver on you promise. A promise, I might add, that I have invested a significant amount in you fulfilling."

"Something came up beyond my control," James stammers placatingly. "More than likely it will still turn up very soon."

I look around the darkness as they speak, my feet rooted firmly in place with paralyzing fear. My heart palpitates rapidly and my eyes are wide with anticipation. I notice Roger's nameless enforcer gazing at me with a dread calm, his hands clasped behind his wide back in a display of quiet strength.

"Oh . . . I am counting on that James, believe me." Roger's voice drops to an icy whisper. "I did not bring you hear so I could 'nag' you. I brought you here to drive a point home."

As he finishes his sentence, he gestures to his companion with a precise flick of the wrist. From behind his back, the fat goon in his tight three-piece suit produces a hardwood baton, and in the same motion brings it crashing down on James' head in a sickening crunch. My old friend lets out a sharp cry of pain and falls to the wet bitumen as his legs give out from under him.

"Jesus Malloy!" Roger exclaims vehemently. "We need him alive you idiot. Why do you always have to crush their skulls like a caveman? You work them over, sure, but shedding blood is a happy accident, not a requirement."

"It might just be a little crack," comes the deep and hesitant voice of the now-named assailant. "Let's check real quick."

Malloy crouches down with an audible groan, clearly having trouble maneuvering his girth in his already stretched clothing. As he turns James over I get the overwhelming urge to vomit. His face is covered in dark red, almost black blood, and more is slowly pulsing out from a jagged crack in his upper forehead. Matted hair is flattened around the wound, and it is not clear to me just how bad his wound is.

"Still breathing boss," Malloy grunts. "Not the worst point I have driven home then."

"Shut up, you gorilla," snaps Roger, shaking his head at the ineptitude of his associate.

"What the hell?" I rasp. "Antiquing is a serious game." Roger looks at me as if I am insane, and then lets out a barking laugh.

"You don't know what the hell is going on here, clearly. I see James has not had the decency to fill you in on how he actually makes a living."

"I am sure he would have soon," comes my automatic response.

My mind is a jumbled mess. Shock inhibits me from sorting the wild notions of James being some "Antiques Gangster" from the explanations that hover somewhere nearer what the truth might be. The one disturbing idea that blooms within this inertia of revelation is that I clearly should not have trusted James as much as I did.

A sobering thought blooms from the back of my mind. *Does this affect the validity of Mr. Montgomery's science?*

"This has nothing to do with antiques, Alan," Roger states flatly. "Call your friend an Ambulance."

My thoughts are still bubbling in a viscous soup of chaotic panic, and the first thing that rises to the surface in a moment of clarity slips out my lips unfiltered.

"I don't have any phone credit," I blurt stupidly, automatically bringing my phone out despite what I have just told him.

"You use pre-pay still? At your age?" comes the surprised response. He looks at me as if I am a child.

"Yes."

"Doesn't matter, emergency services are free," Roger points out wearily. "Hurry up you idiot, he has a pretty bad dent on his head there, you may have noticed."

"Oh . . . I know. Sorry." I stand there manically gripping the firm piece of functional plastic a moment too long for Roger's liking.

"Just make the call . . ." He yanks me close in an explosion of fury, eyes suddenly wide and manic. The feint scent of Trumper's Violet shaving cream drifts ponderously from his neck, lessening the pungency of his sugary breath. I look at him hesitant confusion as he grips my collar firmly. His anger slowly dissipates in the wake of such helplessness. He rolls his eyes, laughs at my distress and pushes me gently away. "I am surrounded by idiots."

My shaking hands flip open the phone and dial triple zero. I press the call button and raise the phone to my ear, counting the amount of rings before the call is answered.

"Police, Fire or Ambulance?" says the detached voice on the other end of the line.

"Ambulance please."

"Please hold while I make the transfer."

I comply, swaying in trepidation and avoiding Roger's icy stare.

"Please state your present location," booms another voice, haughty and impatient. I gush all the information I can, and again in a slower tempo when I am informed of my intelligible speech. Within a minute the operator has informed me that an ambulance has been dispatched and I snap the phone shut with a subconscious action.

A brooding silence develops in the lapse of any conversation. Malloy and Roger just look at me coldly, watching to see if I am going to slip off this narrow precipice of snatched calm and dissolve into a terror-fuelled fervor.

I turn back to look at the club, and wonder if Audrey is even out of the bathroom yet. I cannot imagine a great deal of time has passed, despite the contrary argument my senses are making. From behind me I hear Roger ask, "Ambulance on its way then?"

"Yep," I manage.

"Good boy," comes the response, then a searing pain explodes along the back of my head. I feel my body collapse to the cold, wet road. The impact knocks the wind out of my lungs. A low moan escapes my lips as my vision begins to swim in a blurry haze.

"Much better Malloy," Roger says from what seems like very far away.

Everything goes black.

Drifting

Cardboard limbs slowly drip white paint.

Thin, rusted wires jolt grotesque mannequins under scattered fluorescent beams of light. Flickering shadows dance whimsically around the writhing crude constructs, obscuring clarity with playful abandonment. A virulent, waxen machine billows effluent plumes of purple smoke, chuffing derisively at its slim onlookers. It proudly seeps viscous sludge onto the polished floor, pooling filth around its corroded core.

Gentle laughter sounds from behind me, floating softly past the garish noises reverberating before me. My head follows my eyes backwards as I search for the source of that haunting sound. Rows of decaying red velvet seats stretch far into the darkness before me, cobwebs holding together fraying threads. A solitary spectator is seated calmly in the middle row, white teeth gleaming in a sordid smile. His placid eyes bore into mine with casual ease, effortlessly navigating the depths of my soul. Thin needles of fear work their way up my spine as I shiver in an infantile dread. Reflex overtakes my limbs as I feel my body snap forwards and away from the unerring stare of this secondary spectator.

"Alan," says a voice close to me. "I could do with some pie."

I blink in surprise.

"What kind of pie?" I ask, closing my eyes again, finding solace in the darkness. The world pulses around me as my head sways in dizzy confusion.

"Blackberry."

"Alright."

"Blackberry." The voice repeats.

"Got it, blackberry pie." I exasperatingly confirm his choice of dessert.

"Blackberry."

I open my eyes in frustration. Plain white walls and the quiet thrum of my apartment greet me in a cold embrace. I shift my weight uncomfortably around the hard plastic chair, the soft rustle of my clothing briefly giving an echo of life to the room.

"Blackberry pie," James intones, his gaze anchored to my ambient fireplace as if he has no idea the flames are entirely holographic. Green and orange light pulses sporadically upon the walls, lending some personality to a staid abode.

I notice how imposing he looks in the dim light. Large, brown eyebrows dominate a square face, with his deep-set grey eyes regarding the sparse furniture with barely concealed disdain. His frame looks rather lithe and imposing, but I cannot imagine the government creating obese synthetic constructs.

I nod at him, and get up to satiate his incessant request. The Ease-O-Meal is over by the other side of the room, near the front door and next to the dining table. The floor ripples in liquid protest with each step I take, dragging me down steadily the closer I get to my goal. Soon I am furiously swimming in a sea of white, thrashing against waves of viscid ooze.

My lips part in a primal scream, as I sink further down into the thick milky floor. As I flail my head desperately from side to side in frustrated panic, I notice a severed cardboard arm contentedly bobbing on the surface nearby. It is coarsely threaded in wire that stretches into the brightness above me. My outstretched hands grasp fervently at the awaiting anchor, gaining purchase with clawing desperation. Sharp pain explodes from my shoulder as I am yanked suddenly upwards and out of the swirling eddy. Higher and higher I go, until the room is but a distant speck below me. I look up to see what is pulling me, but I am greeted only with unrelenting brightness.

"Alan," says a disembodied voice.

"Hmmm?"

"Alan," the voice says again, sounding more corporeal this time. "Why are you just standing there looking at the ceiling?"

I laugh. "I don't know James. Not really much to stare at around here I guess."

"Are you going to make us dessert or what?"

"Yes, of course."

I bring up the menu on the screen of the Ease-O-Meal and select blackberry pie with short-crust pastry and a serving of whipped cream. The touch-screen makes a funny tweeting sound as I press the buttons. I don't remember it doing that before.

"What is that noise?" James demands as a burring sound fills the room.

"I don't know. Ugh! Look at that . . ." I shout back at him, pointing to a stream of thick maroon sludge dripping from where finished meals usually apparate. "This thing is broken."

"Nah," he muses. "I don't think they really worked properly to begin with."

The sound of solitary applause softly drifts around the noisy room, audible despite the malfunctioning machine loudly protesting its mistake while sending a slow stream of failed blackberry pie towards the neat white floor. James and I look around in confusion, and I am the first to spot one of the walls slowly parting in the middle to reveal a seemingly endless row of tattered red velvet seats stretching into inky darkness. There is a single spectator, watching us intently in anticipation of our next line. I cast a sideways glance at James and whisper:

"Line?"

He shrugs, and points to the screen of the Ease-O-Meal. Ah! There we are.

" . . .And to prove your velour, you invite the Commander's specter to dinner."

"To make us believe he attended, you put us to sleep with a narcotic," James responds flatly, his gaze flittering around the stage nervously.

"When will we know for certain?"

"Only when it is time to wake," James says with intensity, as he rises from his chair to grip my shoulders. "Are you awake Mr. Febras?"

Displacement

I feel cold.

The sound of quietly flickering fluorescent lighting melds softly with the gentle hum of an artificial breeze. As I hesitantly draw in a lungful of thick air, the smells of stubbornly embedded filth glossed over with astringent bleach attack my senses. Distant voices echo loudly, conversing in sharp tones that briefly cut through the heavy fog of numbness that is gathered around me.

"Mr. Febras?" says a bored voice at my shoulder. If I had the energy, I would have given a little jolt of fear, or maybe even opened my eyes. For the moment though, I simply feel too drained to make the effort. I manage a soft groan, though I am uncertain whether it even manages to escape my lips.

Another voice, more impatient than the first says, "Just leave him, Sandra. We have conscious patients that can use our attention. He will have to wait."

"I guess," The first voice responds, swiftly moving away from my side, the rhythmic swish of her pants and click of her shoes loudly confirm her rapid retreat. I can feel my solitude return in a subtle and comforting embrace, a steady pulsation of quiet contentment sprinkled with situational uncertainty. Curiosity springs up from within this clearer mindset, urging me to open my eyes and confirm my whereabouts.

Brightness invades my vision with immediate intensity as I laboriously lift my heavy eyelids. The weakness that responds to my mind's simple request surprises me, as well as making me wonder just what has caused this near incapacitation.

I blink slowly and squint at the room in which I lay, waiting impatiently for my vision to sharpen the blurred shapes taunting me with their vagueness. Glorious (and previously underappreciated) focus returns triumphantly, lifting the veil of obscurity and letting me know without a doubt that I am at present stuck in a hospital ward.

Outside the improbably clean window at which my weakened head is currently facing, sits a small courtyard teasing me with its inaccessibility. Bright green weeds have defiantly burst through cracks in the beige pavement, lending a feeling of chaos to this otherwise ordered institution.

My imagination takes over as I imagine I am one of those verdant warriors, radiating pleasure at my disruption of the hardened neatness that I have marred. Delicately swaying in the crisp, cool breeze, I marvel at the good fortune and near impossible odds that have allowed me to grow in these unyielding surrounds.

After a few moments, the illusion fades, and my mind can no longer conjure the simple euphoria supplied by escapist absurdism. The sterile room in which I inhabit seems all the more soulless now it again has my full attention.

I hesitantly move to sit up, but find myself hampered by an inadequately sized IV tube that just barely bridges the gap between the cannula and the machine it travels to. I grumble a few curses in frustration at whoever jammed this tube into my arm in such an apathetic manner. As my body slowly lowers itself back to the bed in defeat, my mind begins attempting to recall what events led to this hospitalization.

As I attempt to concentrate more on my flailing thoughts, a flood of confusion drowns my coherence away. I see dim flickering snapshots of memory appear at random, perplexing my mind's eye with their pace and intensity. I experience again the dread of alien machinery surrounding me, causing untold pain whilst a wizened pair of eyes passively follow my progress though hell. The ripple-iron of my ceiling at home hovers in a still-frame above my head, and then I find myself staring at a broken Ease-O-Meal exuding what looks like blood.

The flickering colors of a dance floor light-show work their way into my recollection, gaining pace and ferocity before disappearing as quickly as they came. Audrey is smiling at me now, young, gorgeous and carefree. An overflowing Ibrik hisses at me, spewing foam over an enamel stove-top, just before I find myself closing my office door in a frustrated attempt to gain some momentary peace.

I firmly blink my eyes and try and clear my thoughts, clearly having a hard time separating dreams from reality. I convince myself that the horrible machine-room with the cold eyes does not seem plausible, nor does the strange food-device that seeps thick blood. I think that Audrey is real, or more accurately, I hope that is the case; but there is no unshakeable truth emanating from deep within my mind.

As I begin to again regard the strange apparitions of memory that are lazily swimming around my aching head, I feel strongly drawn to the hypnotically flickering club lights once more.

"James!" I croak loudly as the weight of solid memory crumbles the walls of groggy confusion, washing over my thoughts with crisp clarity. I hear thudding footsteps stop abruptly and change direction towards my room.

"Mr. Febras?" says a weary, yet curious voice. "Are you with us?"

I turn my head slowly towards the inquiry. A middle-aged nurse with heavily applied foundation regards me with a sleepy expression. She has poorly dyed black hair with grey roots painting a silver stripe through the sharp part in her hair. "Where is Audrey?" I ask in a soft voice.

"That must be that near hysterical and quite obviously drunk woman we sent home last night," she responds in a mildly disapproving manner. "She would only let herself be escorted out once we assured her you wouldn't drop dead overnight."

"Is she ok?" I ask, my eyes pleading for good news.

"Well, she wasn't hurt at all, if that is what you are asking. She was the one who rode in with you on the ambulance." The nurse pauses. "She was in a bad state seeing you like that, as you would expect. We sent her home calm enough, told her to come back during visiting hours.

I can't officially say this, but I think you will be able to go home today if the X-Rays show no damage."

"Oh."

She continues in a gossipy tone, "Can't say the same for the man they found you with though."

"James!" I gasp. "What do you mean?"

"His skull was cracked, rather badly." She informs me placidly, her voice turning professional again. "What is known as a Depressed Skull Fracture, which is usually associated with blunt force trauma. Okay? Now he needed to go into surgery as soon as he was admitted so we could lift the bones from where they were causing damage. Alright? The doctor who operated on him is confident he may escape severe brain damage, but his recovery will probably take some time."

"Can I see him?"

"Not possible at the moment. It will be a while before he regains consciousness, and we need to make sure you are ok to go walking about."

"Where is he?" I query, fighting to contain the creeping sense of dread that is slowly spreading throughout my limbs.

"The recovery ward, next to the emergency department, same as you. We will move him to a more comfortable ward when he does not need constant monitoring. You will probably be home by then. For now, no visitors will be allowed."

"Thanks," I manage, attempting to portray a relaxed air. "What time is it?"

"3.15am," the nurse responds automatically, not needing to look at her watch. "Perfect time for you to go back to sleep."

I nod silently as she reduces the dosage of my drip and performs the routine checks before briskly walking off to see her next patient. I wonder how close James' room is to mine. It seems cruel that I will have to leave before getting to see him, despite being such a small distance away from him physically. I close my eyes to attempt to briefly escape my confines, and listen to the quiet and steady thrum of hospital life.

"Alan . . ." says a familiar voice, floating through the air like a ghost's whisper. I turn my left ear towards the sound in a vain attempt to locate it. "Alan." It repeats, and my doubts lessen as to this being an imaginary effect on my tired mind.

"Who is this?" I ask, already knowing what the response will be.

"Who indeed," scoffs the distant, battered voice. "How many people know you are here? Usually, if someone wants to talk to you, they walk up to you and begin conversation . . . I can't walk up to you at present."

Alright, so it was not exactly the answer I was expecting. "James . . ." I begin. "You can be rather convoluted at times can't you?"

"Must be these boring white walls making me extra chatty." He chuckles, his voice distorted with strain. "How are you feeling?"

"Me? I have a headache I guess . . . I will be fine. What about you? How are you even talking to me right now?"

"Ahh . . . the miracles of modern science," he offers elusively. "When I found out the circumstances, I was admittedly rather surprised myself. Still, we are talking, so something went right."

"Alright . . ." I respond with uncertainty. "Let me come and see you face to face. This is ridiculous."

"Alan . . . Alan . . . ever the optimist. It would be best if you just stay put. We are talking now, that is as good as this is going to get for the present. I don't know how long I can keep this up anyway," he says in a taxed, distorted voice.

"Do you want me to get a Doctor?" I ask him tentatively.

"What? I don't know how much they can do at this point."

"They can treat the pain."

"Alan . . . I am so sorry it turned out like this," he apologizes in a strained and somber tone, seemingly ignoring my concerns for him. "I never expected everything to get so chaotic."

"You can never tell what is around the corner."

He laughs sadly. "Yes, but I certainly pushed you around this particular bend, didn't I? You would have been safe if I never convinced you to take this path."

"I don't regret it, at least I think not, anyway. I would have been stuck in that horrible tower if you hadn't offered me a new start," I muse, and there is a short silence. I decide to try and ask how he is doing again. "Is the pain getting worse?"

"Probably," says James. "Can't you tell?"

"I . . . don't think so. I can't really hear you properly," I answer in confusion.

"What are you . . .?" James begins before a loud groan cuts off the rest of his sentence. "Ah shit. Our little conversation is coming to an end old friend."

"James, how can I help end this mess. Get everything back to normal?" A long, poignant silence greets the end of my question, and it occurs to me that he must have slipped out of consciousness. Then:

"You really want that?" he says in a quiet, detached voice.

"Of course, James!" I almost yell in sheer disbelief at his question. "Things just went too far, it happens. Let me sort this all out while you are waiting."

"Alan . . . I . . ." he begins in an utterly defeated tone. "I am so sorry this all went so wrong. You have the key to making this all right again." He yells out in pain again, louder this time and then quiescence returns to the dimly lit ward.

"The key?" I ask myself aloud. "What key?" I have an idea what he needs unlocked, but not where the key could be found. He said I have it? At present, I don't believe my mind is sufficiently sharp enough at present to put the pieces of this puzzle together.

Despite the absurdity of the recent conversation and the weight of events to come bearing down on me, I feel the specter of sleep tugging at my weary brow, lulling me into slumber against my will. As I close my eyes in weary submission, I wonder how long it is going to be until I can properly talk to James and sort this whole mess out.

***

I awaken to the smiling, tear-stained face of Audrey, hovering above me like a weeping angel. My heart flutters in joy as I return the grin and laugh in happy relief at having her so close to me again. She leans down and gives me a chaste, worried kiss whilst hurriedly wiping her eyes.

"Gone for five minutes and this is what you get up to?" she says half jokingly as she pokes me in the arm. "Who did this to you?"

"James' fun friends," I respond, not really wanting to lie about what happened last night. "I know how to get them off his back, how to stop this from happening again."

"Don't be a hero Alan, it doesn't suit you," she says, a worried expression working its way across her features once more. "What are you talking about?"

"I'm not talking tough, believe me," I placate truthfully. "James told me last night that I had the key to what they want. I assume that means the key to his mystical storeroom. I will simply go to work as soon as I can and open the damn thing up. Next time Johnny Gang-land comes around, he can stroll around there and take what he needs."

"Why don't you just open the door and walk away, so you don't have to see him again?" Audrey suggests somewhat sheepishly. "Or . . . something like that?"

"I don't think they meant to kill us love, just smack us into line. That gorilla goon just smacked too hard."

"Let's just . . . talk about this when we get home," she says, trying to push the event from her mind. "When did you say you talked to James?"

"Last night, around three I think. He was being as unconventional as ever and yelling at me from wherever he was laying. It must be nearby," I say as I try and sit up and look around, cursing again at the uncomfortably short IV tube that restricts my every move.

"Honey . . ." she begins with an unreadable expression on her face. "James has been in a coma ever since they brought him in."

Searching

"I must have been dreaming," I say for what seems to be the hundredth time.

Audrey shrugs from behind the wheel, not taking her eyes from the road as we slowly drive through the heavy evening traffic on our way home. "Sounds like it to me."

"Strange . . ." I muse, talking more to myself than at her.

"So you keep telling me," she responds, frustrated at my fixation on what must appear to be a triviality compared to the events that preceded it. "Who cares though, love? What does it matter that you dreamed vividly about Mystical James and his hidden purpose?"

"I still think that despite the fact that the idea came to me in a supposed dream . . ."

"Supposed?" Audrey impatiently interjects.

"I don't know, something about it felt strangely real," I reply, intently sifting through my recent memories. "More real than the stiff mattress that I woke up on, and certainly more real than the glassy stares of the hospital staff."

"Yes, that would be the drugs they had you on."

"It may have been," I say dismissively, "though the point is that the idea that came to me in this *supposed* dream should not be dismissed so rapidly."

"So . . ." she begins in an amused tone. "We have to find a secret key and unlock the old antique store's mysterious storage room?"

"I think so," I hesitantly respond, knowing full well how odd I must be sounding right now.

"Sounds . . . dumb honey. No offense," she says as sweetly as she can manage. The car comes to a quick stop as an impatient driver swerves his shiny, over-priced sports car in front of us without indicating. "Stupid fucking leper!"

"Leper?" I laugh.

"Only someone with their limbs falling off as we speak could be driving that horribly." Audrey scowls, venting her frustration at me at the idiot BMW driver ahead of us. "Anyway . . . I hope you aren't seriously considering getting deeper in the shit with these assholes that cracked James' skull?"

"Getting deeper in the shit with them would require me doing nothing to get them what they need," I argue in a soft voice. "Polite refusals will probably not get me as far as you think, and we will likely fail immeasurably if we try and hide from them."

"This went pretty sour . . . pretty fast," she replies, shaking her head in disbelief. "I never thought antiquing would get you anything other than more free time and maybe a little bit bored."

"Nothing is ever what you think it would be. Reality never seems to match your inflated expectations of it," I state offhandedly, realizing Audrey would have no idea just how poignant that admonishment is.

"I guess that is true sometimes," she admits, shrugging nonchalantly. "But it falls to us to make the most of what the day brings us. You can complain about the shit sandwich someone just threw at your feet, or you can fling it back at them and laugh."

"So I guess you are telling me to throw the shit sandwich back at Roger then?" I slyly grin at the verbal shot in the foot she just fired off.

"Oh! You are impossible sometimes Alan." Audrey moans in exasperation. "I was just trying to get you to appreciate life's ups and downs, not instruct you to go and frolic with gangsters at Sandra's Treasures and Antiques."

"Antiques and Treasures." I can't resist.

"Whatever!" she snaps, suppressing a smile.

"If we want them off our back, we need to give them what they are willing to cave in heads for." My explanation continues after a brief lull. "I saw how Roger looked at that storeroom when he came in on my first day. James told me I have the key for it, so I just need to open it up and this will all be forgotten."

"The key James told you about in your dream?" she wearily responds.

"Maybe it was my memory reminding me through a dream? Or my subconscious telling me what my waking thoughts forgot?" I urge, pleading her to understand my conviction.

"I don't know love. You seem sure, and I trust you," she says as her shoulders visibly sag under the red tint of the traffic light we are stopped at. She looks over at me for the first time since we got in the car. "Can we maybe talk about this when we get home? I just want to revel in the fact that you are still alive for a while, ok?"

"Sounds fair to me, my love." I take her hand and squeeze it firmly. She takes a deep breath in and closes her eyes. A green glow traces her form as the traffic light changes color, and I gently tell her it is time to go.

As we travel in a comfortable quietness, the motor steadily revving and the tires producing an oceanic refrain that never fails to relax me, I begin to reflect on the absolute degradation of what was a smooth and pleasurable reawakening.

It dawns on me that the inherent chaos that provides all the pleasures that I sought brings with it very real and tangible danger. The unhinged and primal nature of society that had been effectively suppressed in my past has not happened yet, if indeed it happens at all this time around. I cannot bring myself, despite what has just happened to me and my friend, to consider this a bad thing. At the same time, I cannot deny how my own explorations in this new life have immediately and strongly affected both my physical and mental security.

Perhaps I am disappointed in the way this new life has worked out for me so far, whilst still reveling in the fact that everyone around me has so many opportunities available to them (and that not all of them will squander theirs like I have mine). It is a frustrating, paradoxical feeling I get when I consider my desire for freedom, and the subsequent aura of dread that surrounds me when I actually attain it.

There are parts of me that cry out for the monotonous security of my previous life, clawing at the walls of my mind in unmitigated panic at the vacuum that has replaced strict obeisance. For the most part though, there is an inescapable feeling of raw promise and potential that hangs thick in the air, ready to punish stupidity as well as reward courage.

Humanity, without the aid of powerful technology, governs itself in a harsh, rapid way. The strong willed and unscrupulous will rule in this era, as they have in times past. The intervention of technology to even the odds and take away individual supremacy over the greater good somewhat stifled what made us progress socially. Social progression, however, was not the goal of the society of my past, rather the controlled evolution of humanity in a structured and designed way.

Give someone an inch, and they will take a mile. So goes humanity when there is even a small amount of personal choice available to them. This is the beauty, and the tragedy of this comparatively chaotic era, as it all depends on how an individual chooses to use their freedom. Where I came from, that luxury (or curse) was taken away from the majority of us so we could not pose a danger to those around us by exercising our right to choose. I remember a jaded worker at my transitional home responding to one of my rants about freedom. They said: *Give someone the right to chose, and they have a high chance of choosing wrong. Better that we do it for them.*

That makes me consider my choice to come back here. It may turn out to be a huge mistake, chasing freedom at the cost of forsaking eternity, but what is important to me is the fact that I had a fleeting chance to once again make my own decision, and I snatched it up.

So what if I got clocked on the head by an angry antiquer? As long as I make it right with them as soon as I can, I will look back on this merely as the shock that jolted me back to my senses in this second life.

To face death so soon from my metaphorical escape from it would be saddening indeed, though I do not think it will come to that so soon. I chuckle to myself in response to the absurdity of the current situation. An undue confidence in the fact that I can bring the matter to a close echoes within the laughter.

"Glad you find this all so funny," Audrey says, unable to stop her own grin mirroring mine. "We're almost there."

Our headlights brighten up the quiet street as she speaks, and my eyes automatically look for the gate to our home. Audrey turns the car into the driveway ungracefully, in a hurry to get out and stretch her legs. We both waste no time climbing out the car and unlocking the house, happy and relieved to again be at home together. I smell the familiar pungency of our huge Peruvian pepper tree as I close the door and go inside, its bold presence reassuring and relaxing my senses with a soothing familiarity.

Audrey flops down on the couch in the lounge room, sighing tiredly and contentedly. I stand at the doorway, admiring her easy mannerisms with a ghost of a smile flickering on my lips.

"What happened to stretching your legs?" I tease.

"I tried that, walking from the car to here," she responds lazily. "I found it was not to my liking at this present time." We laugh tiredly at each other.

"You hungry?" I ask.

"Not really, to be honest."

"Yeah . . . me either."

"I'm just glad you are home love, not really thinking beyond that at the moment," Audrey admits.

"Strange day," I say after a while, filling in the silence with meaningless words.

"I reckon."

I begin looking around the room, discreetly at first, and then with more open intensity. Audrey notices me and sighs in resignation. She doesn't need to ask what I am looking for. I move around the lounge room, briskly running my fingertips over familiar items as if I can somehow sense the anomaly by touch. My lips absent-mindedly let drift a nameless tune as I pick up the pace of my search, going over a rough mental inventory of the room in which I am rummaging. "What is the key?" I whisper to myself.

"A good night's rest, you loon." Audrey sighs at me again, knowing how stubborn I can be when an idea has lodged itself in my mind. "You think if James gave you a key, you might check your key ring first?"

"He has to have hidden from me, so it would only be found in an emergency like this," I say, waving my hand at her dismissively.

"James doesn't trust you?" she demands haughtily. I pause, and look at her searchingly.

"Not as much as I thought he would."

"Or should."

"No." I turn back to the mantelpiece above our fire-place and look with unfocused eyes at the various decorative items that have accumulated there over time. A dusty chocolate tin, a small ebony jewelry box, a pewter candleholder all sit next to various other sentimental and quirky objects. Something catches my eye as I turn away, a new addition to this collective of clutter. A small porcelain elephant stands there, proudly announcing its recent arrival on the shelf by being totally clean. "Hold on . . ." I say, curiosity sharpening my voice.

"What?" Audrey asks in an urgent tone, getting up off the couch and making her way to my side.

"This elephant. James gave me your crappy elephant as a gift, remember? On my first day? I thought it was an afterthought to try and smooth over the rough start I had working for him."

"It probably was," she says as I reach for the poorly crafted porcelain figure. "How is that going to fit in a lock by the way?"

"Wait . . ." I urge, holding up my hand for silence. "Listen." I gently roll the elephant from side to side in the palm of my hand. It makes a soft scratching sound, as if something is scraping along the inside of the figure as I move it.

"Probably just a broken piece of porcelain inside," Audrey says, attempting to convince herself as much as me. "It is pretty cheap looking . . . It wouldn't surprise me at all."

"It is, as you say, cheap looking," I agree, an eager expression forming on my face. "Wouldn't be a real loss if we confirmed your theory, would it?"

"Alan . . ." she soothes. "You really need to lie down for a while I think."

"Nonsense." I laugh as I let the garish elephant slip from my fingers. "I feel fine." It crashes to the wooden floor with surprising speed, making a dull shattering sound as shards of white porcelain scatter along the treated pine.

"What are you doing?" Audrey asks angrily. "I know it was ugly, but that was a gift! More importantly, now we have to clean it up. Wait, no . . . *You* have to clean it up you weirdo."

I am not listening to a word she says. "Audrey."

"What?"

"Look," I say in an excited whisper as I hold up a thick brass key.

Her expression turns cold.

The Key

The silence is palpable.

"Alan . . . what the fuck is that?" Audrey asks in a panicked voice, her hands covering her trembling lips. She looks at me in astonishment, failing to understand my apparent calmness at what I hold in my outstretched hand.

"Looks like a key to me love," I state simply as my gaze drifts from her slowly shaking head to the dull brass key I hold; whose very presence serves to confirm my suspicions and allay my doubts. "I knew I wasn't dreaming."

"You aren't making any sense," she argues, less convincingly than before. "How could you dream up the location of this hidden key? A key that you did not know existed!"

"Dreams may be our minds trying to tell us something we already know, but have forgotten in the mire of everyday consciousness," I say in a calm, reflective tone. My mind feeling clear and accessible for the first time since I woke up in the hospital. "I may have figured this all out without letting myself know."

Audrey looks at me, trying to ascertain how serious I am about what I am saying. I stare back at her with confidence, and her curiosity slowly melts back into fear. "Honey . . . this has gotten too real, too dangerous. Please tell me you are not going to stride back to that shop and unlock it for those mad men. For all we know they are there right now trying to break into the store themselves."

"That door is very, very strong looking," I reason. "Only this key will open it, save the use of dynamite or a high-tech thief."

"So what?' she demands angrily. "Call whoever you need to and tell them you have their key. Call the police and tell them what happened, give them the key.

Anything but rocking up to that place and acting the hero."

I watch placidly as Audrey slowly clenches and relaxes her hands in a physical effort to quell her hot temper. She is standing in precisely the same spot as when I hastily broke the cheap figurine and fished out my prize. I thought she would be relieved to know that I was planning to get this bump smoothed out as soon as possible, so we could go back to living our un-exciting life together.

"You are over complicating things," comes my soothing reply. "As soon as they get what they want, they will not bother me again. Or James. Have you considered that the longer I wait, the more damage they will be doing to James' home and store trying to get in?"

"Big deal! He is the idiot who got himself into this mess. Why should you put yourself at risk for his mistakes?" Audrey asks with a liberal application of incredulity.

"Because he is a friend," I argue, getting indignant at her questioning my morals. I pace back and forth in front of the fireplace, taking care to skirt the shattered figurine at our feet. I pinch the bridge of my nose in frustration and turn back to her questioning gaze. "Surely you understand that I am not the type of person that just abandons his friends whenever it suits me?"

"I know!" she retorts acidly. "You need to be moral and good, even when there is no cause to champion. This isn't a movie, Alan, where the characters are either good or evil and nobody can deviate from their role. When you get killed in real life, you tend to end up staying that way."

Something about her argument strikes me as odd. Audrey, usually a calm and reflective personality (and certainly the voice of rationality in this relationship), is pushing all the panic buttons at once. I suppose my recent trip to the emergency ward might have frayed her nerves, but this is still rather out of character for her. I try and calm down to attempt to persuade her to see things from my perspective.

"You may think this is foolish, but taking the coward's way is not always the smartest direction to take. Fear can cloud our judgment, and prevent us from seeing things as they really are." I pause, hesitant to inform her of the choice I have just made "This will all be over tonight."

"Tonight!" she screams at me. "You can't wait to save the day can you?"

"This isn't some hero complex," I argue. "I don't want James' life ruined by one little slip up. It can be prevented, so why not prevent it?"

"He is probably not as innocent as you make him out to be." She laughs bitterly, turning on her heel and making a show of calmly examining the dusty knick-knacks arrayed on the mantelpiece. "No wonder he wanted you with him at that store of his. Someone to protect him with their noble nature, maybe?"

"You are not being fair," I say, finding myself overcome with dizziness of a sudden. I shakily pull the nearby computer chair out from under its desk and sit down unceremoniously. I gather my thoughts in silence as Audrey stands rock-still with her back towards me. Closing my eyes to the swirling eddy of recent memories and current revelations, I try and concentrate on convincing Audrey of the prudence of this plan. "It is just a quick visit there tonight, love. I can call them when I get home and tell them the door is unlocked and they can take what they need. I won't go back to the store after that until James is back, except to lock it all up again. The whole process won't take a day."

"Alan . . ." she moans in exasperation, as she turns back to face me. "Nothing is ever as simple as it seems."

"I know," I tell her, nodding my head in brief acquiescence. "But these last couple of days have been so chaotic, so utterly outside my control that I need to . . . I don't know . . . snatch some solidarity back from the world."

The irony is certainly not lost on me, who up until recently, had cried out in angst at how drab and ordered my life was. It is well and good, I suppose, craving the pertinent bliss distilled from riding waves of chance and uncertainty, but that enjoyment is somewhat lessened when you begin to drown in the very waters you sought to tame.

My lover says nothing, closing her eyes in anger at my stubbornness. I watch in muted curiosity as she lets out a slow sigh and lowers herself to her knees, bringing her face close to mine. I feel her hot breath tingling the raised hairs on my brow, our souls touching for a brief moment through a pure emotive connection.

Her bitter anger slowly evaporates as a potent sadness breaches her core and overtakes her waking thoughts, spreading steadily like a virulent plague. I watch her burden with a heavy heart, realizing how afraid for me she must already be without the extra burden of watching me walk out the door so soon after returning home safely.

She opens her eyes and they are full of tears.

My world turns cold. I grip the arms of the chair in white-knuckled restraint, trying my hardest to ignore the horrid numbness that has overtaken me.

"Stay with me tonight?" she asks in a hollow voice. "At least give me that much."

I do not respond, not knowing what to say or how to let her down gently. She tries to hold back a sudden sob, and it catches in her throat. The noise hits me like a physical blow. I reach out and pull her to me. She latches on, abandoning any pursuit of emotional restraint. Hot tears stream freely down my shoulder, warming my frigid body as she cries loudly in my ear. I feel her fingernails fiercely clawing into my shoulders, as if by holding on as tightly as she can I will never leave her side again.

"Why are you doing this to me?" she asks pleadingly. "Just let me have you here a little longer. I don't want to go back to the nothingness that surrounds me when you are not around."

"What are you talking about?" I ask in a raw and questioning voice. "Nothingness?"

"I need you here," she repeats urgently, desperately trying to convey the importance of her words. "Without you I am nothing."

"It's not that bad," I stammer in open astonishment at the notion of how attached to me she appears to be. "What do you do when I am at work? When I am asleep? You don't need me that much. Nobody does."

"This is different. Can't you see?" she exclaims, showing no signs of calming down. I cannot remember the last time I have seen her so unnervingly sad. She kneels in front of me, soul laid bare before me in stark detail. I drink her sorrow into my brain, reeling from its sickly fumes with labored breath. In brief flashes of clarity, I attempt to grasp at the reasons behind her sudden anguish, and to the validity of her hysterical state.

She lifts her head suddenly, her eyes boring into mine. The imploring strength of her gaze demands absolute attention. "If you don't come back to me, I cannot go on living."

"Why on earth wouldn't I come back?" I ask in bewilderment, rubbing my temples in ferocious anxiety. I lean back in the chair in an attempt to force a feigned posture of calm, hoping to perhaps project some measure of peace to ease Audrey's battered mind. I take a few steadying breaths and attempt a lighter tone. "Those guys would not gain anything from killing me."

She looks at me in an expression usually reserved for the rather dense among us, her incredulity cutting through her sorrow for a brief moment. "You have the key, Alan. Not them."

"Yes . . ."

"It is your choice," she whispers.

"I . . . know." I cannot keep the condescending tone from creeping into my response.

"No, I don't think you do. You don't have a clue what is behind that door do you?" she says in a defeated monotone.

"And you do?" The feeling of being in over my head returns with rapidity. I look at Audrey, her eyes red with fallen tears and wonder how much she knows about what is really going on.

"I have a bad feeling about it, Alan. I want you to believe me when I say that nothing will be fixed by you opening that door."

I narrow my eyes and regard her questioningly. What is she going on about?

"What have I done to upset you?" she asks in a pleading voice. "Why can't you just forget about this crap for one night and stay by my side, where I need you to be? Doesn't it feel good to be home? To be together again? I would never have left your side at the hospital if they hadn't kicked me out. I finally get you back and you want to leave me again?"

I falter as her words cut through my shallow bravado with a surgical precision. What am I thinking? How could I just walk out the door and leave her alone again while I go on some fool's errand that can clearly wait until morning? The importance of my task becomes more trivial with each passing moment that I absorb her pleading expression.

My eyes wander around the room, objects blurring out of focus as my vision swims in uncertainty. The numbness that overtook me when Audrey broke down fades away as I reach out and hold her close to me. For a long while we are lost in this warm embrace, not needing to put into words our quiet contentment. No questions are asked, no answers demanded. It is a peaceful, fulfilling moment.

But it doesn't last.

Audrey begins to feel cold in my arms. As each second passes, I find it is getting more and more difficult to savor the aura of insulation that was feeding our appeasement. I lift my head back and regard her calm expression.

Something seems amiss.

My heart sinks in resignation as the weight of the small key in my hand begins to steadily dilute her persuasions. Audrey's enfolded limbs seem to grow steadily cooler as I steel myself for what is to come.

"The sooner this is done, the sooner we can move on." I say as I gently move her away from her and stand up, slipping the key into the front pocket of my jeans. I reach for my faded brown leather jacket and try and ignore the huge well of sadness building up the further I move away from her. I slowly put on my soft leather gloves, delaying the moment when I have to tell her I am leaving.

"You have made up your mind," Audrey whispers, stating the obvious in a broken voice. She stands up and turns to me with a blank expression. "This didn't last very long, did it?"

"I don't know love . . ." I respond gently. "What didn't last long?"

"Our time together," Audrey states flatly. "Our time together since you came back."

"From the hospital?"

She doesn't answer, looking at me numbly in acceptance of the unavoidable. I try and smile at her, to ease her woes by showing how little I am worried myself, but all that comes out is a strained grimace. I take a deep breath and pick up the car keys from the desk, the metallic clinking sending an unavoidable shiver down Audrey's spine. A single tear rolls down her face, and I follow its progress down her curved cheek, rooted to the spot in shameful remorse. I find the willpower to move again once it fades away from sight.

"Bye love," I say in the calmest voice I can manage. "I'll be back soon."

She slowly turns away from me and steps over to the couch. I watch as she slowly lowers herself down onto it and clasps her head with rigid hands, breathing deeply and silently. I cannot make myself approach her, knowing how little it would help her at the moment anyway.

"I'll be back soon, love," I repeat gently as I trudge slowly to the front door.

As I turn the ancient iron handle and shiver as the outside breeze hits me with icy relish, I swear I hear her whisper:

"No. You won't."

A Feeling of Dread

A heavy blanket of silence envelops me.

I gently lay a black-gloved hand on the key that I have just slid into the ignition, delaying the moment where I must actually start the car and imbue the surrounding stillness with mechanical life. The dim moonlight illuminates my hot breath as it turns to steam in the cold interior, forming condensation on the glossy windshield.

As I clench my jaw tightly and close my eyes for what seems to be the tenth time this minute, I have to remind myself that I am sitting here through my own volition. Reality, as usual, is proving to be far less congenial than what was suggested in the realms of my imagination.

Just go over there and unlock the door. I think to myself. *Simple as that.*

Right . . .

Why did I have to leave straight away? I know my arguments seemed sound as they cascaded out my fluttering lips in front of Audrey, but as I sit here in solitude I notice that the echoes inside my head reverberate much more forcefully than usual. Yet despite these ominous feelings saturating my waking mind, I can think of no tangible reason to abandon my pursuit now that I have begun it. I am probably just jumping at shadows, as I suppose everyone must be guilty of from time to time.

I shrug suddenly, as if to loosen the heavy shroud of fear from my hunched shoulders and bring life back to my motionless limbs. Mentally grasping at the brief flash of energetic confidence that surges through my awaiting arms, I turn the engine over and flick on the bright headlights. In front of me, our small tin garden shed glows bright like the sun as I flood the area with light. I blink slowly, taken aback at the sudden illumination after so many minutes skulking in the scant light.

Taking a steadying breath, I put the car into reverse and slowly back out the driveway. Every crunch of gravel and bump in the road seems more pronounced in the dead of night, and I am glad to hear the more dominant sounds of the revving engine as I pull away from my house. As I drive steadily towards my destination, I notice the roads are eerily void of any signs of life, be it car or pedestrian. Even on a weekday, there are usually some signs indicating that you are not the only human being in existence.

The car's cabin is still cold as ice, and despite pawing at the heater controls for a few long minutes I find that I cannot make myself any warmer.

"This car is a bloody fridge on wheels," I say, recalling that Audrey and I had dubbed our white Toyota Camry Wagon "The Kelvinator" for its looks as well as how cold the engine stayed on even the hottest of Australian summer beach journeys. A flicker of a smile appears on my lips before I recall the state I had left her in mere minutes ago. I muster all the willpower I possess to try and push the image of her pleading, tear-filled eyes from my mind. When I come back successful in my endeavor, I can explain to her how we won't have to worry about any troubles like this ever again.

The yellow glow of street lights trace the outline of large eucalyptus trees as their leaves flitter in the strong autumn breeze, while the sprawling fields that hastily pass me by are peaceful in their darkened placidity. This relaxing scenery soon gives way to the garish display of suburban sprawl, which means I am no more than half an hour away from the city, and thus my destination.

Two pinpricks of light appear in my rear-view mirror, and I let out a small exhalation of pleasant surprise at finding another car accompanying my lonely trek. Its headlights grow steadily larger as I follow their approach, and I easily deduce that the driver behind me is certainly in a hurry.

Before long, my interior is flooded from behind in the harsh glare of the other car's high-beams. Despite this being a two-laned highway, the driver behind me begins to repeatedly sound his horn in an attempt for me to get out their way.

"What an obnoxious jerk," I mutter to myself. "What, is he waiting for a break in the fucking traffic?"

For a long couple of minutes we travel in an awkward tandem, their horn cutting through the silence at random intervals. This prompts me to slow down incrementally, to try and persuade the annoying (and most likely drunk) driver to change lanes in frustration. It briefly crosses my mind that his maniac might be trying to get me to stop for some reason, but I do believe that ship sailed as soon as their insane behavior started. I am not going to let Audrey's prophecy of doom fulfill itself.

A heady mix of frustration and panic at the absurdity of the situation coax my heart to beat considerably more rapidly than what I would usually enjoy. I grip the steering wheel and try and force patience into my younger mind, but I feel wisdom is slowly losing the battle over the surging adrenaline pumping unceasingly around my body. Before I can prevent myself from doing something stupid like slamming on the brakes, the annoying tailgater decides that now is a great time to move into that second lane and continue his urgent journey towards a collision with a tree.

"I guess the phantom-traffic has cleared up . . ." I say to myself in a relieved tone as the car passes mine. I snort in confusion as I notice that the vehicle that caused all this angst looks exactly the same as my own. A white, mid-nineties Toyota Camry station wagon. It is too dark, and the car is going too fast for me to glimpse into its interior and discern weather it was indeed my car and I am not simply walking very fast holding a steering wheel pretending to drive. I chuckle to myself at the prospect as the rear-lights of the near identical car fade into the distance.

Peaceful solitude drapes the road once more, and I am left reflecting on the diminished mental capacity of some people, as well as musing on the prospect that their driving instructor must have passed them to relieve the blood curdling fear they experienced when taking them for a lesson.

I turn on the radio and rapidly flick between the stations, frustrated at how much all the music seems to sound the same. It is not long before my ears are once again treated to the low swoosh of my tires on the damp road, and not much else. I begin to relax slightly for the first time since I shattered the figurine on the wooden floor of our cottage home, letting the absence of most external stimuli massage my fears into temporary submission.

Something odd in the distance draws my gaze like a magnet to its juxtaposed presence.

As I draw nearer, driving at a steady speed, time seems to slow as the horrific reality of what I am approaching crashes through the walls of my psyche like a bullet. Before me, is the crumpled shell of the car that harassed, and then overtook me not minutes before.

There is no doubt in my mind as to the chances of survival for whoever was driving this now wrecked car. The only person walking away from this crash will be the weary policeman slowly shaking his head from side to side.

The notion that I had secretly wished for this bastard to end up wrapped around a tree does little to ease the shock of seeing my wish turn into stark actuality. I feel no triumph, no hidden joy at this person meeting their end because of their own idiocy. All I feel is sorrow.

I am close to shedding a tear at the ruinous carcass of metal and bloodied flesh as I draw nearer to the scene, yet I do not let myself succumb to breaking down over a stranger's demise. This misery I feel must have something to do with the fact that I still have not seen another car on the road besides this one, and this fellow traveler has been mutilated in a horrific display of careless abandon.

There are no flashing police lights to console me with an authoritarian air, no nervous onlookers clutching their heads in shock to share my disbelief. There is just this dead stranger splattered over the damp bitumen and me.

Nobody else.

Once again I find myself reaching down to the hidden reserves of willpower I never knew I possessed in order to find the strength to continue down this path that I have chosen. I let my mind take over the mundane tasks needed to keep the car heading in a straight line while my waking thoughts get lost in a slurry of shock and confusion.

I tear my eyes from what looks like a premonition of my own demise on this very road, and attempt to write off this whole thing as an uncanny coincidence. How many people would have seen the same car as theirs in an accident? Probably a lot.

Don't over-think it, just focus on what you set out to do tonight . . .

My hands tightly grip the steering wheel as I grit my teeth and speed up, fleeing the scene of destruction. I can't bring myself to call triple zero and inform them of this travesty. Disassociating myself from what is happening seems to barely manage as a coping mechanism at present.

The Main North Road stretches out in front of me, still bizarrely devoid of life, and I focus intently on my own problems in an attempt to blot out the tragic coincidence that I am leaving behind me. For a few minutes, I pass through time without any signs of company.

Then I see it.

Two pinpricks of flickering light appear in my rearview mirror, growing in size with alarming rapidity. As they approach me, I see fountains of sparks streaming out from underneath the stuttering headlights, as if a portion of the approaching car is scraping along the ground. A dark thought crosses my mind, before I dismiss it outright as pure fantasy. I look straight ahead and try and ignore the sporadic brightness that is suddenly flooding my cabin. This, of course, proves an impossibility, and I find my eyes looking back to see what kind of disturbance this might prove to be.

My blood turns cold as I regard the reflection in the rear-view mirror. A crumpled Toyota Camry station wagon is somehow following me, and I have no doubts as to this being the same one that I had just passed mere minutes back. Its smashed headlights are somehow emitting a staccato of invasive light as they approach my rear bumper at an unnervingly steady pace.

"What the fucking shit?" I exclaim to myself. "There is no way this is happening." Yet happening it is. No matter what I say to myself, the car behind me creeps ever closer in a horrific display of impossibility. The wreck I passed was in no way able to drive away from its own carnage, yet here it is behind me.

"Oh yeah?" I scream hysterically. "Let's see how you keep up with a non-totaled car!"

I press the accelerator as hard as I can. There is, admittedly, not much response from my four cylinder station wagon, but I do notice the speedometer begrudgingly acknowledging my efforts. Despite this, the abomination following me maintains a steady speed. Panic overtakes rational thought as I fail to comprehend the twisted reality yawning at my heels.

Surely I can outrun it?

One hundred and thirty kilometers per hour.

One hundred and fifty.

Nothing changes. The car behind me effortlessly matches my vain attempts to pull away from it.

One hundred and eighty.

My engine starts to protest being pushed to such high limits, and the peripheral blur from the side windows is beginning to make me nauseous.

This is not working. The ominous presence looms behind me like the specter of death itself, calmly keeping pace with my frantic attempts to evade it. Surely the mangled corpse that is likely still sitting behind the wheel is equally indicative of the personification of my demise? I close my eyes for a brief second in a moment of pure concentration.

This makes no sense . . . Surely this cannot actually be happening?

When I open my eyes again, the car is gone.

I mentally steel myself in the wake of such a sudden absence. Minutes drag by as I let the tangible reality from outside my windows confirm my sanity restored.

For a long while, the only sound my ears choose to register is the loud and labored breaths that I cannot seem to willingly placate. The idea that I was simply imagining the horrific encounter solidifies as I regain a semblance of composure again.

I am not long away from Sandra's Antiques and Treasures now, so I hesitantly decide to continue on my original journey. The last portion of my drive is characterized by furtive glances in the rear-view mirror and an overly tight grasp on the steering wheel.

The road is still amazingly bereft of life, and as I turn down the side street that James' little store sits on, I regard the surrounding businesses with a confused glance. Between now and the last time I drove down this street, all the storefronts have been boarded up or vandalized in a bizarrely encompassing manner. I slow down to a crawl as I regard each and every abandoned store in absolute amazement. Cafes, pubs, advertising firms, and handbag outlets are uniformly empty.

"Seriously . . ." I whisper to myself, "What the fuck is going on?" I push on, watching as my headlights illuminate one abandoned business after another. Bizarrely, as I reach my intended destination, I note that Sandra's Antiques and Treasures is entirely intact. Not a broken window or kicked-in door to speak of.

Righto . . .

I sit in the car for a while, trying to make even a little sense of has happened to my surrounds since I involuntarily visited the hospital. I notice a dampness permeating my shoes, and I look down to find my feet submerged in a pool of blood.

"Ahh . . . Fuck!" I scream as I grasp for the door handle. I recoil in shock as I discover the door to be nothing more than a mass of crumpled metal. Tears well up in my eyes unbidden, as a deluge of panic washes over me. I lift my feet from their bloodied rest and ferociously kick at the driver's side window in an attempt to escape this mangled prison. The glass does not give in to my attacks, seemingly impervious to my fury.

"Just! Let! Me! Out!" I scream in time to my kicks. Cracks appear as I voice my rage, and with a few more determined kicks it shatters with relative ease. Quickly, I scramble out the window and rush to the sidewalk outside of James' store. I scream. Primal and raw, my voice reverberates upwards and into the nothingness above me.

I stagger around in bewilderment, looking back at the crumpled wreck from which I have just emerged. It is identical to the mangled car which I passed on Main North Road, except for the trail of blood that leads back along the road I have just travelled.

The faded yellow door of Sandra's Antiques and Treasures beckons me to come and turn its chipped metal handle, inviting me to shut myself inside and be insulated from the insanity that is currently surrounding me. I find, though, that I cannot move. I am welded to the spot with the uncertainty and doubt that comes from the unique notion that you just drove a crumpled wreck thirty kilometers to a newly abandoned street, let alone the fact that you passed your dead self on the way.

My legs collapse from under me, and I cover my eyes with my hand. My thoughts swim in a mire of dizzy nausea.

Come clarity . . . I think to myself. *None of this makes any sense.*

Why don't you open your eyes and see the world for what it really is? You could not have possibly driven a wrecked car all the way from Gawler South. There is no way all these stores are suddenly abandoned in the space of a few days. You are making this up. You are stressed.

Open your eyes. See the world as you should.

I slowly comply with my own commands, hesitantly lifting my heavy eyelids, then managing to lower my hands from my face in shaky submission.

My hollow laughter echoes in the empty darkness.

Disorientation

Nothing has changed.

I look around slowly and it sinks in that what I see before me is real. My lips let out a grunt of bestial shock as the wishful optimism I was harboring moments before melts away under the glaring presence of reality. Queasy uncertainty scatters the last shreds of calm from my thoughts as the realization that I am not hallucinating hammers into my psyche. There are no stress-conjured phantoms harassing my tired thoughts, nor is there a specter of fear distorting truths with a taut hand. There is merely this surreal panorama before me, demanding my attention with grasping forcefulness.

The surrounding world is abandoned.

My car is a twisted, bloody wreck.

I feel like I am drowning amidst surging tides of uncertainty, and I cannot seem to find solid ground in which to pull myself up and recover. Nothing makes sense, and I feel a heady panic blocking my every attempt to rationalize with deft ease. The only clear direction my mind is giving me is to escape the street. To hurry up and get away from this abandoned, horrible place where clouds of fear cling to every shadow.

My eyes dart around, absorbing every detail hundreds of times over. I try my hardest to disregard the steadily growing pool of dark red blood from beneath the crumpled white steel of what used to be my car. I attempt to ignore as best I can the heavy boards that cover every window and door as far as I can see.

Everywhere, that is, except James' Antiques store.

My footsteps echo loudly up the empty street as I break into a run. Cold water from the asphalt below me splashes up my legs, an icy grip that encircles my ankles as I reach the chipped yellow door. The streetlights nearby flicker a faded orange bloom over the doorway, illuminating my destination in a hesitant display. I notice as I briefly look over my shoulder that the street behind me seems to darken as if the moon has disappeared behind a cloud.

I look up.

Above me there is only darkness. An endless void without stars to guide.

I feel my limbs shudder involuntarily as my eyes widen in shock. Is the true face of this universe that I have been sent to revealing itself at last? I study the darkening street around me in frenzied determination, as if I can somehow absorb some hidden truth in the fading light. Nothing answers my hasty search but panic. Whatever is happening around me, I am damn certain it would be best to be removed from it.

A low wind blows quietly past my ears, and as I feel its cool touch on my exposed flesh, I am overcome with a feeling of hopeless dread. Wasting no more time, I force my limbs to obey my mental persuasion to approach Sandra's Antiques and Treasures. As I reach the entrance, I pull of my gloves and throw them to the damp ground so I can easily grasp the key for the front door.

My heart beats ever faster as the heavenly sound of a lock clicking open drifts gently upwards to my waiting ears. I leap quickly through the doorway and slam the battered door shut behind me. I stand there in the darkness, still as a post, breathing heavily as adrenaline surges throughout my body.

The store is deathly quiet. No ominous wind flirts with my fearful thoughts here.

I reach to my right and fumble for the light switch. The room floods with fluorescent light as I slam all the switches on.

I regard the store before me in open joy. It is just the same as when I last saw it. The shelves are admittedly as abandoned as before, but that is because I never got around to cleaning them. Calm descends, allowing me a brief respite from the surrounding madness. Here, in the relative safety of this familiar room, I begin to address the last half hour in my mind and attempt to gain some solidarity over the events.

The notion of phantasmagoria that I had regrettably abandoned in the crux of fear begins to feel approachable again. I gain the courage to turn around and look out the windows but I only see a reflection of myself and the store behind me. Of course. That is normal I guess, seeing as these lights are so bright in here. I clumsily wave at my mirrored counterpart and turn back to the store.

My heart still races at a pace that is quite distracting, so I attempt to spend a few moments focusing on restoring a state of relative peace to my rattled nerves. My damp feet take their first steps in minutes, but they show no signs of warming up as I meander aimlessly around the store. Odd.

I pick up an old snuff tin from a nearby shelf and turn it over in my hands absentmindedly as I look around at the assorted curios nearby. I notice that I am having trouble tracing the delicate embossed scrolling with my fingers, so I move to take my gloves off. As I look down to my naked hands, I drop the tin to the floor in a yelp of surprise.

Why am I so numb?

Letting the renewed tides of panic guide my actions, I move over to a dusty seven-day straight razor set and wrench open the decorative burl lid. With no time between thought and action, I snatch up the closest ivory handled razor and flick it open. It is a gorgeous Damascus blade coated in a light sheen of oil that has prevented any corrosion. Much like most other things in this store, it is well preserved but abandoned.

I stall for a few moments, and then run my thumb gently down the edge of the blade. A feint scratching sensation tingles my flesh in the place of sharp pain, and my heart skips a beat. Blood wells along the newly formed cut, and begins to run down into my palm.

It feels cold.

I throw the razor across the room and it clatters away under a dusty shelf displaying dozens of glass candlesticks. I hastily make my way to the register whilst knocking over antiques that have likely not been disturbed in decades. My cut shows no signs of healing, and as I stand there with my arms limply at my side, blood begins dripping freely to the scratched wooden floor.

Once again, I attempt to glean understanding from what I see before me, head darting from side to side like a caged animal. My vision swims in a blurry haze, and I rub my eyes clumsily to try and regain focus. As I slowly lower my hands, I notice with unmitigated panic that it is not my strained perception softening the edges of my surround, but the objects themselves loosing definition.

It is as though this universe is collapsing.

What was moments before a safe and cozy place to be now feels like an airtight prison slowly suffocating me with each snatched breath.

Heavy doubt turns fluid limbs into granite, making every move I make harder than the last. Yet my waking thoughts compel me through strained, yet undeniable reasoning, to turn around and leave.

As body complies with mind, waves of fear crash upon the delicate walls of my resolve.

I move to the door, trying to ignore the coldness steadily creeping upwards from my still saturated ankles. My bloodied hand reaches for the handle . . . and finds nothing. I look down to see if my hand is indeed touching the handle and I am too numb to feel it.

"Fuck . . ."

There is no handle with which to grasp.

I stagger backwards and regard what I thought was the exit. A flat panel looks back at me, hastily painted like a stage prop. I kick as hard as I can at the supposed door, and it doesn't move an inch. I look at my whitened reflection in the store window, and move as close as I can to my mirror image so I can look past it into the darkness.

Nothing.

I turn off the lights as quick as my numbed body allows, and expect to see the street suddenly appear when my pale reflection vanishes.

Blackness.

The same void into which I stared as I regarded the night sky is now inches from my nose. It is infinite in its depth, a darkness that seems to suck all the life from around it. It is terror incarnate, the face of oblivion.

I must escape it.

My hand once again slams down on the plastic surface of the light switch.

A crackling of electricity pulses around the room, skittering like a thousand bugs trapped within the walls. I wait impatiently, teetering at the precipice of madness.

The sound gets louder with a sudden determination, then stops.

Darkness drapes every corner in a heavy curtain, uninterrupted by my pathetic attempts to allay its steady progress. I back away from the window and bump into some sort of metallic pot in my retreat.

I search around me hoping to catch a glimpse of light, no matter how small. Desperation is all I feel, its cold fingers plucking each separate nerve in my body as though they were strings on a guitar.

After slowly retreating to what I believe to be the center of James' store, an influx of hope surges through me as I see the most welcome visage in my life. A glint of metallic blue light is slowly moving around a large surface, refracting and morphing as I approach it.

I draw nearer, barely navigating past the objects jutting out of the shelving at random intervals.

"Stupid fucking junk."

My objective is in front of me now, and I realize what it is with a sudden understanding. The darkness from behind me looms high, an entity far more sinister than a mere absence of light.

I don't care about that anymore.

A nervous chuckle works its way from my smiling lips as I reach for the small brass key in my pocket. I know that I have no other option but to open this door, but I still find myself hesitating.

I wonder if what I believe to be behind the door will be matched with reality. I even manage a faint hope that what awaits me will not be detrimental to my desires. Did James have any idea know how this door would affect me in the end? I recall his nervous smile trying to mask the deep fear at what was locked away here, and of what would happen if Roger got his hands on it. The more I turn it over in my mind, staring hypnotized at the metallic sheen in front of me, the more I begin to doubt he has actually been through this door himself.

How could he have?

The time for reflection draws to an end as the air around me becomes deathly still. Staying here would be boring, to say the least. Nothing you can really do in an empty room, besides leave it I suppose. A resigned air drapes my shoulders as I take a final steadying breath.

The heavy metal lock opens with accommodating ease.

"Righto."

I turn the handle and start to pull the door open.

An Open Door

An explosion of white-hot fire propels me backwards and onto the sticky floor.

Leathery arms slither around my torso, locking me in place as I weakly try to sit up. My eyes strain to regain focus, but I am too dizzy from the shock of the blow. Warm blood pools around me, trickling from an agonizing cut in my arm.

"Alan!" cries a voice from a great distance, echoing a thousand times around the crisp white walls. It sounds familiar. "What the hell happened here?"

My lips fall open to deliver a response, emitting a slurred whisper that does not even reach my own ears. Weakened limbs slowly curl in frustration as my head turns to stone, protesting every attempt to turn towards whoever is addressing me.

The rabid voice cascades around my ears in volcanic intensity, demanding and frantic. My tired mind drifts away in a gentle breeze of apathy, leaving the plumes of discontent billowing furiously beneath me.

An unceasing drone of mechanical discontent reverberates throughout my core, apathetically reaching for undivided attention.

Watery yellow droplets rain uniformly sideways past immobile arms. In a searing flash of orange, they morph into hot, dancing sparks whirling in a chaotic spiral that floats ever upwards to the sagging roof. Pulses of unyielding brightness cut through the muted fog, blinding my searching vision with sharp agony.

I drift amidst the plains of my shrinking awareness, reality becoming an abstraction that no longer seems worth exploring. My eyes stay closed longer each time they black out their surrounds. Weak lids heave against the invisible threads of fatigue that bind them tightly shut.

I feel my heartbeat slow with each strained breath as the pool of red in which I lay grows colder on my skin.

I do not mind.

A creeping decay writhes around me, crumbling pristine surfaces with steady progress. The leathery arms that encircle me hold me in a tight embrace, no longer an enemy, cradling me in absolution towards my final destination.

I close my eyes to the mundane, memories taking place of the rot and destruction before me. They soothe me, caressing my weary mind with gentle apathy. A peaceful darkness creeps up from within me, soothing my broken body with a studied hand.

"Alan!"

You can't deceive me anymore.

"Stay with me!"

Tendrils of smoke amplify the scent of burning flesh as I slowly inhale. Raw screams of agony surround me, cutting through my descent into finality. Emotions lull my eyes open with a forceful temperance as my flailing memory rescues your final moments from the permanence of death.

Temporarily.

My lungs swell with their final breath, taunting this doomed vessel with the elixir of life made obsolete. Cracked, parched lips flicker in a ghost of a smile.

Oblivion caresses me, her cold fingers soothing the dull pain that permeates my every limb.

I welcome her touch.

CPSIA information can be obtained at www.ICGtesting.com
Printed in the USA
LVOW090733070612

285039LV00002B/188/P

9 781618 971814